TALES OF A
SIXTH-GRADE WERECAT

Book 2:
The Cat's Grimoire

A.M. DEESE

This is a work of fiction. All characters and events portrayed in this novel are either products of the author's imagination or are used fictitiously.

TALES OF A SIXTH-GRADE WERECAT: THE CAT'S GRIMOIRE

Editing and typesetting by Kingsman Editing
Illustrations by Megan Corley
Cover art by Shivana Brhamadat
Typography by Joel Torres at Driven Digital Services

First Edition May 2022
ISBN: 978-1-957412-01-6

www.amdeese.com

This book is dedicated to Cat Jack.
I love you to the moon and back.

Contents

Chapter One

It Ain't Easy Being Kitty

O nce upon a time, I didn't believe in witches or magic or anything like that. And then I turned into a werecat.

I guess that's all changed now. If you're anything like my friend Jay, you probably think being a werecat is pretty awesome. And sometimes it is, but I just wish he would see that it's not always as cool as he thinks. For instance, he's never woken up with an actual hairball, and he's never found little black hairs wrapped around that little hangy ball thingy in the back of his throat. Not cool.

But being a werecat also makes me faster and gives me cool reflexes and heightened senses. And it helped me get Ethan to stop picking on me. Oh, and it kind of got me a girlfriend . . . so I guess, in a way, being a werecat is the best thing that's ever happened to me.

I hate it when Jay's right.

Even though it's a Saturday morning, I'm in a rush to get downstairs and wolf down some breakfast before I go to Miss Gray's house. I stop by her place a few times a week after school, but Miss Gray said I should start giving her my free Saturday mornings as well. Mom is thrilled about my new "job," but that's only because she doesn't know that Miss Gray is a werecat . . . just like her son.

I wonder if that's something I'll ever be able to share with her. Probably not. I can picture it now—Mom converting the upstairs bathroom into a giant litter box. Yeah, right. Can a human's head actually explode? Because her reaction would probably be something like that. Yup, definitely not a secret I'll be sharing with Mom anytime soon.

Mom is at the kitchen table frowning into a mug of coffee by the time I finally get downstairs. "You'll be late," she says without looking up. "Did you separate your laundry like I asked?"

"Aren't you supposed to be at the open-air market thingy?"

She smiles, her warm brown eyes meeting mine. "Don't change the subject. Laundry. Now."

I resist the urge to roll my eyes. Mom has eyeballs in the back of her head, I swear. So, I puff out my chest and head back up the stairs.

"And the market is next week!" she calls after me.

Like I can be expected to keep up with all of that. Mom is busier than I am. And between track practice, homework, after-school gaming sessions with Jay, and lessons with Miss Gray, I've been way busier than I'd like to be. I've barely had any time to call Mckenna, and it's been nearly two entire weeks since she's given me her number. I've just been so busy, I remind myself as

I kick all my discarded clothing into one giant pile on the floor. That's why I haven't been able to reach out to Mckenna — because I've been busy and definitely not because I'm too nervous.

After the laundry is more or less sorted into two piles, I drag the baskets downstairs and deposit them in front of my mom with a wave of my hands like it's raw salmon on a platter.

"Now can I have breakfast? You know, child labor is against the law."

She rolls her eyes as she pushes herself from the table and reaches for my first basket. "I'll send a report the moment there's a child being labored." She makes a face over the contents of the basket and walks across the kitchen to the laundry room. "Do you have time for eggs and bacon, or do you just want to get a bowl of cereal since Miss Gray is expecting you now."

It wasn't phrased as a question, so I go to the cupboard and grab a granola bar and a bag of chips, a well-balanced breakfast, in my opinion.

"Chips? Honestly, Felix. Well, at least get a juice box from the fridge." She shakes her head.

Ugh, juice box. Like I'm still a toddler. But, ooh, Tropical Tangerine?! My favorite. I snatch up two and meet Mom's eyes.

"What time will you be home?" she asks me.

Good question. Miss Gray said we had to begin training

for the "darker sides of the gift," whatever that means. "Er, a few hours?"

"Take your time. Lola and I were thinking of driving into the city and stocking up from that discount fabric store I like. Are you going to Jay's this afternoon? He's welcome to come over for dinner, but you make sure you're home in time. I feel as though you've been too busy for your poor mama lately."

"Uh, I'll ask him. I'd better go. I'm already late."

"But don't be late for dinner."

"I won't."

"And don't forget to remind Miss Gray of her invitation to dinner this Friday."

"Okay!" I yell back over my shoulder, finally making my way out the front door. I snap it shut firmly behind me before Mom devises some other useless thing for me to do. Mom has been inviting Miss Gray to dinner every weekend for the last month, but Miss Gray always finds some excuse not to attend. Not that I'm bothered by that. The forced lessons are enough Miss Gray interaction for me, thank you very much.

The sun has already set its mind to baking everything under it, and I think the bottom of my sneakers are beginning to melt into the pavement by the time I make it to Miss Gray's gravel drive. She opens the door before I am even halfway up the walkway and beckons me forward with hurried hands.

Right, I'm late. I'm not so sure why it even matters since I've never seen her do anything or go anywhere, so I can't imagine my tardiness is disrupting her schedule.

"Felix." She nods at my appearance and gestures for me to sit at the dining room table. Most of our lessons begin there.

"I've a mind to get you a wristwatch, young man."

"Uh, yeah. Sorry. Mom had me doing a few — "

"I see. So it was your mother's fault. I thought perhaps you had overslept after last night's escapades."

Dang. She notices everything.

Maybe I can talk my way out of this. "I was just practicing. Like you suggested."

Miss Gray shakes her head. "I instructed you to practice control, not to gallivant the neighborhood streets like some feral tomcat."

Nope, not talking my way out of this one. At this point, it's best to keep my mouth shut and look apologetic. After a few moments, Miss Gray runs out of steam and sits beside me with an exhausted sigh.

"Until you've mastered your powers, you put yourself and others at risk. That is why it is imperative you take this seriously. Your induction into the werecat society comes with many responsibilities. Nod your head, boy, so it at least appears like you're listening."

I bob my head up and down enthusiastically.

Miss Gray doesn't often roll her eyes, but she does now. "Felix, I need to know that you are mature enough to continue forward in your training. The world is still much larger than you know."

"I've visited my grandparents." I mean, it's not like I'm Jay and I've never left Alabama. I have grandparents in Boston and Italy. I have a passport and everything.

"I don't mean big in that sense, at least not entirely. There are so many dangers in this world, more so to werecats. Dangers from other . . . forces."

"Like werewolves?" I try to keep the excitement from raising my voice. Jay and I have been dying to learn more about werewolves.

"Mmm, yes. Wolves and other Weres and other more sinister forces as well." She coughs into a tiny purple handkerchief she must have had stuffed up her sleeve.

"Other sinister forces? What could be scarier than a werewolf?" This time I can't help the curiosity hiking my voice up.

Miss Gray looks away, her hand reaching for the silver talisman hanging from her neck. All werecats have one, but the type of material it is made from can vary wildly from werecat to werecat. It all depends on what matters to that individual. Mine is an old Jackie Parker Jr. baseball card.

I reach for the card in my back pocket, and as always, the thin plastic burns hot in my hands. The familiar face peers back up at me, the eyes focused just behind me. JPJ and his perfect pitch.

"Miss Gray?" I prompt when she doesn't respond.

"There are many things," she finally answers, then abruptly leaves the table and the room.

Am I supposed to follow her? Miss Gray is always creepy, but she is being especially strange today.

"Felix, there are many sides to your bestowment that you still have yet to discover. Many aspects of your gift are wonderful and should be seen as the blessings they are. But . . ." She swallows, sliding an old leather book onto the table between us. "There are also some darker sides to this magic of ours. This grimoire will serve as a practical lesson plan for what's to come."

"Whoa. Now hang on just a minute. You've had an instruction manual this entire time?" She could have shared this with me weeks ago! I mean, there was the time that I got stuck as the cat because my baseball card was in the washing machine. And I still don't have the hang of how to get down from a tree.

"Oh dear. I can tell by your tone that this information is upsetting to you. I never mentioned the grimoire before because you hadn't completed enough of your training, and you weren't ready."

I take a few deep breaths, working to clench and unclench my fist. Okay, so Miss Gray hasn't purposefully made my life more difficult; I just hadn't been ready before. I can accept that. But I have been pushing myself lately. And haven't I learned a lot over the last couple of weeks?

"And now I am?" I stretch my arm across the table, reaching for the old book. "I guess I've finally mastered the basics enough to try some more advanced cat skills?"

"No."

"No? But I—"

"Felix, this isn't a game. Kittens devote years to their studies before mastering their skills, and you've a long way yet. Your introduction to this book has nothing to do with your skill level."

"But you said—"

"I said you were not ready, and I meant it. The book is . . ." She sighs, frowning down at her hand over the old leather. "The book is also dangerous, Felix. But it's our only resort. The book will help keep you safe."

She pushes it toward me, and suddenly I'm not as eager to touch it.

"Keep me safe from what?"

She ignores my question and leaves the table. I watch as she walks into the kitchen and pours us both a tall glass of milk. I accept mine and take several sips without any objection.

"After your milk, please shift into the cat for further instruction." She looks tired.

"Miss Gray, keep me safe from what? Other Weres or . . ." I trail off when her golden cat eyes meet mine.

"Hunters. Were hunters who will stop at nothing until they find you."

Chapter Two

More Magic, More Problems

"Hunters? Hunters! And why would they want me?"

"Not just you. Any werecat. And the wolves. Or any other sort of Were for that matter."

I take a moment while it all sinks in. Hunters. People who hunt people like me. I swallow hard.

"Finish your milk, Felix."

I'm not so thirsty anymore. Miss Gray seems to understand because she doesn't ask again and instead opens the old book to a seemingly random page. The musty odor of stale leather hits my nostrils as she frowns down at the words written on the page.

"Hmm. No. Certainly not. A simple protection spell is what I need." As old as Miss Gray is, her fingers should be gnarled and wrinkly, but she flips through the pages with ease. "There. This will do."

I get up from my spot at the table so I can peer over her shoulder. The book is written in English, although some of the words are misspelled, and the cursive is something awful to try to sort out. I shake my head at the contents and try to ignore the goosebumps on my arms. It's only because it's cold in her house, not because I'm scared or anything like that.

A protection spell? Like a magic spell, the sort that would come from a witch? I swallow at the thought. "Umm, Miss Gray? What's a grim war?"

"The grimoire? Well, a book of spells, of course. Oh, we'll need moon water. I'll be right back. There's some in my pantry."

She leaves me standing at the table staring down at a book

full of magical spells that didn't exist just moments ago. What sort of person has a book of spells if not a witch? Miss Gray returns moments later with a spray bottle. She mutters some strange words over my head and then sprays the water right in my face.

"What the heck was that for?" I yelp and jump back, wiping my face with the bottom of my shirt.

"I just told you, the protection spell."

Suddenly I remember all the rumors surrounding Miss Gray, and I wonder if three weeks is long enough to decide if someone is an evil witch or not. I have to ask, even though I don't want the answer. "So it's true, then. You're a witch?"

"Me? A witch? Because of a bit of magic?" She chuckles. "No, I'm not a witch, and never you mind how I came by this book if that was going to be your next question. All you need to know is that it did belong to a witch at one time, and now it belongs to me."

"But if you're not a witch, then how can you use magic?" I scratch my head at the thought.

"We werecats are creatures of magic. Of course we can wield it. But be warned, while you can use magic, you are also more susceptible to the dangers of it. Magic is a two-sided coin. Wonderful and dangerous and not to be taken lightly."

"Cool. So when do I get to try it?" I'm totally learning how to shoot a fireball.

"Young man, this is not a toy, and you will not be 'trying it' or even so much as be in the same room as this without my permission. You have no idea the depths of the dangers this grimoire holds. It's so much more than a simple compilation of spells. There is knowledge in here that is worth dying over." She smiles. "Now, come here so I can show you this." She picks up the book, and I follow her to the bookcase. When she places the book on the shelf, the book  disappears. Miss Gray reaches into the empty space, and the book materializes back in her hand as she pulls it from the shelf.

"That was totally freaking awesome." Seriously. I want to slide it on and off the bookshelf a few times, but Miss Gray points back to the dining room table and leaves the grimoire.

"Yes," Miss Gray says solemnly. "It is very awesome and very dangerous. That book must never be removed from its shelf. I'm only showing it to you so you will know of its location should you ever find yourself in an emergency. I don't want you to touch it if I'm not around."

I nod, uncomfortable with the intensity in her eyes, but Miss Gray shakes her head.

"No, I need you to say it. Promise me you won't touch the grimoire. Not ever."

"Not even to put it back on the shelf? What if you forget it out, and I'm just putting it back?" I can't resist asking. Like, does she seriously expect me just to forget that this book of magic exists now? Why did she even show it to me?

"I would never. This is the point I'm trying to get into that thick skull of yours. There is nothing more dangerous than this book. It's more than just a list of spells, more than just a daily account of one powerful witch's life. The spells in this can be used for good, but they can also be used for ill intent. Why, there's even a spell that can take away your induction, rendering you back into a mere human boy."

It takes a moment for her words to register. Werecats are cursed to shift every night under the light of the moon. The only thing that can prevent this change is their unique talisman. It's what saved me over the last few weeks. Even after I discovered my talisman was the baseball card, I had nightmares for days, worried I would somehow lose it and be forced to live out the rest of my life as the cat every night. But now Miss Gray is talking about some new thing that can just take all that away? And even worse, it's something she could have done to help me this entire time? If my induction into werecat society was a mistake, then why didn't she just change me back that first night? Did she enjoy watching me suffer?

I take a deep breath and feel my fingernails digging into my palms. I take another deep breath, but it doesn't help. I'm both sweaty and cold. There is a sudden buzzing sound in my ears and another pounding in my chest that I think might be my heartbeat. There are so many things I want to ask, but my tongue feels too big for my mouth. Am I starting to shift without realizing it?

"Why did you lie to me?"

Miss Gray seems as surprised by the question as I am. "Young man, I have been nothing but forthcoming with you since you have been inducted. An induction, I will remind you, that came about entirely as a result of your own actions."

"Yes you did! You let me believe I would be stuck as a cat if I couldn't find some mysterious talisman. That my entire life depends on this!" I take the baseball card and pinch it between my thumb and pointer finger, waving it in her face. "What if I didn't find it so quickly? Would you have just let me change into a cat every night without even caring? All this time, you could have fixed me, and you let me believe I was in danger of —"

She roars. Not hisses or mews like a cat. Miss Gray roars like a lion.

The baseball card slips through my numb fingers, and we both watch it slowly flutter to the polished wood floor.

"Felix, I have never lied to you, and I never will. But you will treat me with the respect I deserve, especially while in my home, and most especially while I instruct you on matters of life and death." She narrows her eyes at me and places her bony hands on either hip. "Now, are you ready to hear an explanation about hunters or do we need to waste more time?"

I'm still mad enough to chuck her precious grimoire into the trash bin but I nod. Throwing a temper tantrum won't get me any answers. I once again take a seat across from her at the table.

"Excellent. As I was saying, the book and its contents are not meant to be taken lightly, and the anti-talisman is just one of the more potent spells. There are secrets in there that could break this world."

I make a tiny "oh" sound as all the breath rushes out of me.

Miss Gray nods briskly. "Indeed. Which is precisely why it would be irresponsible to display its contents around snarky adolescents who have a problem listening to instructions. Your teenage hormones probably already have your powers in check." Her eyes soften. "I'm sorry, Felix. This is not how I planned to engage in this discourse with you, but certain events have pushed my actions."

"Hunters."

"Yes, hunters. But with proper preparation, their threat can be nullified. And while the grimoire is one of the tools available to you, Moon willing, it's not a weapon you'll need to access unless as a last resort. I'll explain it as best I can. I mentioned that Weres are creatures of magic. Whether cursed or inducted, the magic creates the Were and destroys the human."

"You make it sound as if magic is alive."

"Oh, it is. Very much so. And remember what I said about magic being a double-sided coin? There must always be balance. There are those who are born with magic. Beings with inherent magical abilities, like witches. And opposing them, hunters. Beings who acquire magic by siphoning from others. It has always been this way."

"But why do they want to capture us? Do they have some science laboratory where they perform all kinds of crazy experiments?"

"No. They capture you, drain the magic from you, and discard your body afterward."

Oh. I let that sink in. Suddenly I don't feel like making jokes or getting angry about the book anymore.

A quick snap of fingers in front of my nose brings me back to the conversation at hand. Miss Gray scowls at me. "Young man, are you listening? Repeat everything I just told you about the upcoming lunar eclipse."

"Umm, I might have missed that last part."

"A total lunar eclipse is a rare and magical sight. Even more so for a Were. But it can also be a very dangerous time for our kind. You see, just as the eclipse will supercharge your abilities, it will do the same thing to hunters. Once again, there must be a balance to the magic. Weres have an innate magical camouflage that protects them from a hunter's sight. But, during the lunar eclipse, a hunter's gaze will be opened, and they will be able to see you for exactly what you are. All Weres, once hidden by the moon, will now be revealed. Hunters can always be a danger, but it is only during a lunar eclipse that we are truly at our most vulnerable to them."

Ghostly fingers seem to trace a path down my spine, and I shiver from the sudden goosebumps all over. I didn't like the idea of being vulnerable to anyone, but especially not to some group of crazy magic witch people who enjoy hunting people like me. Once again, I have to ask, even though I really, really don't want the answer.

"And let me guess, we have to start preparing now because there's going to be a lunar eclipse soon?"

I swallow at Miss Gray's grim nod.

"I'm afraid so. A total lunar eclipse will happen in three months' time."

Chapter Three

The Boy Next Door

There isn't much to say after that. Miss Gray asks me to change into the cat, and we run through some agility drills before she waves her hand in a dismissive gesture and announces that we can finish for the day. Finally. It's late in the afternoon, but a quick peek at my driveway shows Mom's car still isn't home, so I decide to stop by Jay's house. Dr. Kim answers the door with a warm smile. Jay's parents are both doctors, and his mom has been my pediatrician since I was born. And yes, it's as embarrassing as you can imagine. After some awkward small talk, she releases me to run down the hall to Jay's room.

Jay is crazy smart and annoyingly organized, so I can only blink in surprise at the disaster that greets me when I open his door. Jay sits in the center of his carpet with piles of books and loose papers stacked in a semi-circle around him. Mixed in with that are three calculators, his tablet, a half-dozen fun-size candy bar wrappers, and an odd assortment of curved glass balls and magnifying glasses. He looks up at my arrival, squinting in confusion.

"What time is it?" he asks by way of greeting. He looks around at the mess by his feet and starts stacking the books atop one another.

I shrug in response and throw myself back onto his bed. I'm still sweaty from my training session, so I grab the remote for his ceiling fan and dial it up to full blast.

"Bro!" Jay leaps to his feet as papers fly everywhere, and I hurry to turn off the fan with an embarrassed grin.

"Sorry, buddy." I reach for a paper that somehow made it up to the bed and hand it to him. "What are you working on?" We've only been in school for, like, a month or something, so I can't imagine Jay brought all this out for a homework assignment.

Jay shoves to his feet, awkwardly juggling the glass orbs. "I entered the state STEM fair. I'm building a telescope to study the effects of the moon's craters on the Earth's atmosphere."

What? I hope he doesn't honestly expect me to understand any of that. And who builds a telescope? "Miss Gray said that werecats have magic powered by witches and that I have three months to learn how to be a proper werecat before hunters come for me."

"Witch hunters?"

I hush Jay and quickly explain everything I've learned. Like me, my best friend is most interested in the idea of werewolves. I wonder if they stand up on two feet like some fuzzy rage monster or if they simply turn into big shaggy wolves like the werewolves in Twilight. Then I wonder if vampires exist and make a mental note to ask Miss Gray next training session.

"So I guess this means, with all your new werecat training, you don't have as much time for the channel, huh?"

Jay and I run a YouTube channel for Minecraft. We almost have one hundred viewers now. We've almost doubled viewership over the last two weeks, and there's no way I'm losing momentum now.

"Nah, I got it. We'll be fine. Besides, Miss Gray says I'm invisible to hunters until the eclipse. I don't think there's much to worry about."

Jay doesn't seem like he believes me, but I shrug it off and pick up one of the strangely cut pieces of glass from his desk. "So this thing makes a telescope, huh?" I peer through the curved orb, smirking at the distorted image of my bare feet on his carpet. My toes shrink and then grow larger depending on the angle. "Neat." I spin in a slow circle, noting the swirl of distorted images beneath the glass until a movement outside Jay's window catches my eye.

"Hey! Someone is moving into the old Johnson house." I lift my chin toward a moving truck backing into the neighboring driveway. The Johnson house has been for sale all summer after

Mr. Johnson took a job offer in Florida. I toss the glass onto Jay's bed and pretend not to notice him wincing before going to the window to give the new neighbors a more careful look.

Jay shoves up next to me, and we watch as some old guy climbs out the driver's side and begins pulling things from the back of the truck. He and another guy pull out one boring item after another. An old chest, a couple of bed frames, an antique dresser . . . yawn.

"A bike! They have kids, right?" We haven't had a new kid move to the block in, like, six years or something, so this is possibly the most exciting thing to happen since Mrs. Cremshaw threw up all over her desk last week. Her entire class was dismissed early to the gym so the janitor could get things cleaned up. Jay said the room still smelled, even two hours later.

We watch the window, but the slow unloading of the truck gets pretty boring after a while, so Jay and I decide to record a session for YouTube before I have to head home for dinner. We film for thirty minutes or so before we hear the doorbell go off. Jay and I exchange a glance, then he pushes to his feet and walks to his door to peer down the hallway. He's barely poked his head out when his mom yells something at him in Korean. Jay grunts back—he says his Korean accent is embarrassing—but then beckons me forward.

"Mom says we should come out and meet the new neighbors. They have a kid our age."

Power of perception. Can't get anything past me. Jay and I exit his bedroom, me trying not to run and Jay half shuffling, half lingering back behind me. I thought that maybe Jay was starting to grow out of his old habits of being shy around new people. I guess not. I resist the urge to roll my eyes at my friend and instead turn toward the front door, pasting a big phony smile on my face that is sure to convince all the adults in proximity that I'm a friendly neighborhood kid, certainly not a troublemaker.

The smile leaves my face. Is it possible for someone to smell funny? Not with stinky armpits or gym shorts — I mean . . . well, funny. Tiny hairs rise along the back of my neck and seem to tickle down the length of my spine.

I'm not sure what it is about this kid, but I instantly hate him. I think his haircut is lame, and I don't like anything that he's wearing, even though it's something I've worn myself. I want to punch him in his stupid face.

"Hi." The kid grins and holds out his hand. He is taller than both me and Jay with long legs and skinny arms. His face is narrow, and his big brown eyes seem magnified beneath his glasses.

"Hunter, this is Felix. He lives across the street. And my son, Jay." Jay's mom reaches behind me and pulls Jay toward her. Jay gives me a strange look as he shoulders forward. "Boys, say hello to Mrs. Muridae and her son, Hunter. He'll be starting at the school on Monday. Be nice."

Is it just me or does Dr. Kim look directly at me when she

says that?

I reach forward to meet Hunter's hand in a friendly shake, but at the last moment, I knock his hand away from mine in a strange reverse high five.

"Felix!" Dr. Kim sounds embarrassed. Mrs. Muridae laughs and says something about boys and their secret handshakes, but I tune her out as I stare at my fingers. My hand definitely did that all on its own. And is it my imagination, or are my fingernails growing into claws? I clench my fists to hide the change and shove them both behind my back.

"Want to come to my room? We were just about—"

"Let's go outside!" I can't explain it, but I am desperate to get as much space as possible between me and this kid . . . and yet somehow I also want to get closer. I'm not sure what it is about him, but I have this odd feeling in my stomach like I just ate a bad burrito. And I still can't figure out his smell. It's pungent and wrong. I don't like it, but also, I'm curious to smell more. Maybe he accidentally took a bath in gasoline or something. I'm not getting locked in a room near him. I grit my teeth, almost choking on my saliva as the cat's canines lengthen in my mouth. I lick my lips, and my tongue feels rough and course. Not now. I focus on my talisman and struggle to calm down. "I need some fresh air."

Thankfully, Jay doesn't fight me on this. "Er, yeah. Hunter, is your bike good to go? We can show you around the neighborhood. I mean, if that's okay with our moms."

Jay's mom responds. I think Hunter's does, too, but all I can do is focus on my shoelaces.

Stop freaking out. Your talisman is in your pocket. You

won't turn into the cat unless you want to.

And that's the problem. I do want to turn into the cat. More than anything. I want to become the cat, pounce on Hunter's face, and shred it to pieces.

Chapter Four

Being Neighborly

I'm not sure who leaves the entryway first. I stumble after them, ignoring the odd look Dr. Kim throws my way. So much for making a good first impression on the new neighbors.

The late afternoon sun is blinding, hitting the street at just the right angle to get us all in the eyes. I mumble something about going to put air in my tires and cross the street toward my garage. I haven't felt such a surge in my powers since I first got them, and I don't like the feeling. I need to be in control of the cat at all times.

I use the time away to get my breathing back to normal. Something weird just happened, but I'm not sure what. Probably I need to go and talk to Miss Gray about it, but I don't want to get another lecture on the responsibility of the cat. I take a few deep breaths through my nose and out my teeth, the way Fitz yells at us to do during drills, and it seems to help. My heartbeat slows down. I tune out Jay and Hunter's small talk and focus on what I can smell. The Sawyers just mowed their lawn, and Mr. Brewer is brewing coffee. Okay, good. Normal things. I take another deep breath. Jackie's painting her nails . . . and there. That smell again. It's definitely coming from Hunter.

I can feel him staring at me, almost as if he knows what I'm thinking, but that's an impossible thought. I try to ignore him staring at me and make a show of pumping air into my tires. They're full already, so I only waste a few moments before I'm wheeling my bike back toward them.

"Felix, Hunter used to live in Boston. I told him about your grandparents." Jay smiles at me, and I force myself to smile back. I need to talk to Jay about the weird vibes I'm getting from Hunter, but I need to do it alone.

"I used to live in a lot of places," Hunter says. "We, umm, move around a lot."

"Well hopefully you get to stick around a bit longer this time," Jay says, oblivious to the fact that I'm trying to meet his eye. We're supposed to be best friends. You'd think he'd be more observant. Sheesh. At least the smell seems to have gone away. I wonder what it could mean.

"Yeah, moving is lame." I inhale deeply, testing for any unpleasant smells, but the sensation seems to have passed.

"Well thanks for offering to show me around, guys. What is there to do around here?" Hunter does a slow circle of the houses along the cul-de-sac. "It seems kind of quiet."

"You mean boring." Jay grins. "And yeah, it kind of is. Not much to do out here except ride on the trails or post up at the arcade." He shrugs. "I don't even know what I'm missing out on anyway. I've never even left the city. Not like Felix here."

"Yeah, so Boston? What part do your grandp — "

"Why do you guys move around so much?" I interrupt.

25

The question seems to leave my mouth all on its own. "I mean, isn't it weird timing? School started a month ago."

Hunter looks uncomfortable, and I'm glad the question catches him off guard. I don't think I've ever instantly disliked someone so much. Not even Ethan, and he's my mortal enemy. Or, at least he was.

Jay glares at me—oh sure, now you want to make eye contact?—but I ignore him and stare at Hunter, waiting for an answer.

Hunter's shoulders rise in an awkward jerking motion. "I'm not sure. You'd have to ask my dad."

That buff military dude still unloading boxes? No thanks! I toss my head, hoping to shake off these weird feelings, but if anything, they only intensify. The longer I'm around Hunter, the more I don't like him. "It's because your family is running from something, isn't it? What's your secret? I— " I slap my hand over my mouth before I say anything else I regret. I mean, sure there is something off about this guy, but I don't want him to know that I think that.

Hunter takes a step forward, and I notice, not for the first time, that he is quite a bit taller than I am. He might have glasses and a scrawny-looking head, but his legs are long, and his arms seem to have enough reach to pack a punch. "Secret? My family doesn't have any more secrets than the average person on this street." Okay, I did not make up that look he just gave me. Does he know that I'm a werecat? Is Hunter an actual . . . hunter?

"Yeah, so weird that Felix cares about that." Jay's hand comes down on my shoulder, and he shoots me a look that says,

Dude, what is your problem?

I shake my head so quickly, I give my neck a case of whiplash, but Jay drops it, and thankfully, so does Hunter.

"So, there's some good trails out here? Wanna show me some before my parents realize I'm not helping them unpack?" Hunter is all smiles again, and I realize he's making a peace offering. Now's the time to squash any lingering weirdness between us. I mean, sure, there's definitely something off about him, but I need to talk to Jay and Miss Gray about it first. Especially if Hunter is a Were hunter.

I step forward to lead the way. There's no reason not to put on a friendly face so long as he does.

Jay relaxes and straps on his bike helmet with a big grin. "Sweet. Let's show him Jackson's Leap." He straddles his bike. "Hunter, you'll love this path."

I force a smile and try to relax. I just need to make nice for a bit longer. At least until I can figure all this out.

"Hunter, start up at the center. The trail gets thin toward the middle." I gesture out to my side, and Hunter approaches me with a nervous smile.

He has a right to be nervous because as soon as he is close enough, my leg stretches out and trips him.

Chapter Five

A Dangerous Catnap

I think I may have just been possessed. No, seriously. I don't know how else to explain it. One moment I'm trying to make nice, or at the very least trying to give the impression that I want to make nice, and the next thing I know I'm sticking my foot directly in Hunter's path. I manage to catch him thanks to a certain set of cat-like reflexes. Hunter jerks out of my grasp.

"Okay, that's it. Are we seriously going to have problems? What's your deal?"

I wish I knew. I open my mouth, but my brain is too slow to come up with an actual excuse. Jay lifts his eyebrows at me, but I can't sputter anything out. Finally, Hunter makes a sound of disgust in the back of his throat.

"Whatever, man. Just forget it. I need to get home and unpack anyway." He hops on his bike and leaves me and Jay in the middle of the street. I'm still staring after him when Jay grabs my shoulder and pulls me back toward him.

"Hello? Felix, snap out of it!"

Huh? I slowly blink Jay into focus. There's an odd

humming noise vibrating in my head.

"You're freaking me out, man. And you're growling."

The humming noise stops.

"Want to tell me what that was all about?" Jay looks more concerned than angry. I feel the heat rise in my cheeks, and I wish I could blame it on the late afternoon sun and not the complete embarrassment of my recent actions.

"Jay, I . . . I wish I could explain. I just don't like him."

Jay snorts back a chuckle. "Well you made that very obvious. To everyone. I don't get it."

"There's something off with him." I quickly explain the strange surge in my powers and the loss of control of my body. "I think he might be a hunter," I admit.

Jay rolls his eyes. "A hunter named Hunter? Seems a bit obvious, don't you think?"

"No, that's actually the perfect disguise if you think about it. And it would explain why his family moves around a lot. Come on, you have to admit that at least that part of the conversation was a little weird."

"No more than you growling at him as he walked away."

"Because the cat didn't like him!"

"The cat?" Jay frowns. "Felix, I thought you were the cat."

"I am." But I don't feel so certain. I have never felt so out of control before. "I think I should just head home. I'm tired." I'm not though. My heart is beating so fast, I feel as if I've just finished racing Ethan around the track.

Jay looks skeptical, but he doesn't argue. "Yeah, okay. I'll see you Monday."

"What about tomorrow?" Sunday afternoons are for livestreaming. Jay cuts off any protest with a quick shake of his head.

"My parents are making me go to Jackie's recital. It's so far away, Mom is packing a cooler. But I'll try to stop by when we get back." He hesitates, like he wants to add something else but isn't sure how to word it. "Maybe you should talk to Miss Gray?"

He isn't wrong, but I can't bring myself to head back to Miss Gray's house for the second time on a Saturday. I mean, how many lectures and weird experiences should a kid have to go through on the weekend? Instead, I shut myself in my room and lie on my bed. It's easy to calm my racing heart when all I have is crown molding to look at.

Once I feel somewhat normal, I heave myself up into a sitting position. My talisman hangs out of my basketball shorts, and I pull it out to frown at it. It doesn't look any different. It's not even hot to the touch like it sometimes gets after it's been used. Could Hunter actually be a hunter? The idea is no stranger than me turning into a cat.

A few weeks ago, none of this stuff was even possible. Sheesh, things change quickly after fifth grade. Wouldn't it be nice if the only problem I had was whether or not I should call Mckenna? And I can answer that now — I definitely can't call her. What would we even talk about? My cat powers? The fact that I think the new kid belongs to a family of dangerous hunters? Maybe I should have gone and talked to Miss Gray, but a part of me is mad at her too. She liked to say that she didn't lie to me, but for someone who was supposedly an open book, she still found ways to constantly surprise me. Like that spell book, her grimoire. I still don't know what to make of it. And her big reveal of witches and magical eclipses . . . it's a lot to handle.

So is Hunter an actual hunter? I'm not sure, but one thing I'm certain of is that he poses a danger to me.

I throw the baseball card on top of my wrinkled sheets and walk to my window. Mom must have come in here and opened it before she left for the market. She's constantly yelling at me to pick up my room or at the very least "air it out." I can smell the autumn blooms from the rose bush in the front yard. My senses don't seem heightened anymore . . . at least I don't think. My nose wrinkles at the thought. Stupid Hunter. He and his giant of a father run boxes from the moving truck to inside the multi-level brick home. His mom sweeps the porch while classic rock blares from a stereo in the living room. They seem normal, but everything inside of me screams that they are not. Miss Gray said

Weres are invisible to hunters before the eclipse, "hidden from their sight revealed by the moon" is what she actually said. I'm not sure what that means. Ugh. I'm gonna have to go back to Miss Gray's tomorrow, aren't I?

I sit back down on my bed and pick up my current reading assignment. Maybe something has gotten into me. The story is just boring enough to have my eyes blinking, and suddenly a quick nap before Mom gets home seems like a wonderful idea.

I'm asleep almost as soon as I close my eyes and instantly dreaming. I know it's a dream because even though I'm walking like a human, I am still aware of my tail. It swishes back and forth behind me as I rotate in a wide circle. In the distance I hear a high-pitched giggle, but I can't find its source or anything else for that matter. I'm in the intersection of a series of hallways. A stretch of white wall greets me in any direction. If the weird setting isn't enough to creep me out, that maniacal laughter certainly is. I take a deep breath and clench my fists. My hands are my own, but my nails have lengthened into sharp claws, and two pointed canines dip just over my lip. I have always imagined that this is what a werecat should look like, something scary and dangerous, a more powerful version of me. When in reality the cat is more kitten than anything else.

"Where am I?" I'm not expecting an answer, but that same wild laughter echoes back to me from up the hall. If I were awake and in the real world, I would probably never walk toward the sound, but that's exactly what I do.

The hallway forks up ahead, and I turn left without thinking. This new hallway seems identical to the first. No doors, no artwork, just plain white walls over a plain tile floor. The hallway ends abruptly. A dead end. But that would mean . . . I swallow. A maze?

The giggle sounds closer, reverberating off the walls.

I turn around, but the hallway looks completely different. It's just a dream, I remind myself. Don't panic.

There's a distant banging noise, the sound of a door slamming shut. I tilt my head, straining to hear more.

A hand clamps down on my shoulder, and I'm woken up by my screams.

Chapter Six

Werecat, Grounded

My bed. I'm in my bed. I'm safe. I sit up and blink rapidly, struggling to regain focus and shake off any remnants of my dream, er, nightmare. But it was just a dream, and everything seems to be fine now, even if my head does feel a little funny. No, the important thing is I'm fine.

My momentary relief is dashed almost immediately when the door to my room flies open, and Mom steps in. When her eyes meet mine, her gaze turns thunderous.

"Felix!"

Why do parents need to be so dramatic? Honestly, she is screaming at me like I'm not standing here right in front of her . . . wait a minute. I'm standing . . . on the bed? I look down and yelp in horror at the sight of furry paws. How did I turn into the cat?

Why did I? I spot my talisman on the bed beside me and give myself time to feel another small dose of relief. Okay, well at least I haven't managed to somehow lose it! But why did I change? It's not even a full moon.

Mom enters the room, marching toward me.

"Felix!" she screams my name again. "Get in here." She utters a string of curses in her native tongue that would make my Noni wash her mouth out with soap. Uh-oh, I can see where this is going. Mom isn't a fan of animals in the house, and I think she's got some sort of grudge against cats because she's forbidden me from ever owning one. She wasn't too pleased the last time she caught me lingering around in cat form, so I need to make a quick exit before Mom forces an eviction.

She freezes. Her brown eyes are bigger than silver dollars, and her skin seems to kinda lose all of its color, all at once. Slowly she backs toward the wall and screams.

It's the most terrifying sound I've ever heard. Mom is like the bravest person I know, and to witness her in such total panic, I can only imagine what she sees. Have the hunters found us? Or worse, has she discovered I'm a werecat?

Mom screams again, and this time I realize her attention is focused just behind me. I turn around, and for a moment, I don't see anything.

A flash of white fur leaps from my bed and races across the carpet. Suddenly, that's all I can see.

A rat.

Catch him! Get him. Capture the fur. Grab the fur. I NEED to make him mine. I jump from the bed and chase after him. We run in circles around the room. I think Mom continues to scream, but I can't hear her anymore above the frenzied beating of my heart.

The rat manages to claw its way up my curtain and escape out my open window. Oh no, you don't! I jump out the window after it.

I forgot I live on the second floor. I just barely manage to latch onto a nearby hanging branch. This isn't the first time this tree has aided in my escape. Unfortunately, I only manage to get enough of a grip to slow down my fall because, seconds later, my claws lose traction, and I drop the rest of the way onto the lawn. The grass is slightly damp and pokes the pads of my feet like tiny soggy needles. And there is no sign of the rat.

I catch a quick glimpse of Mom's angry face before she snaps my window shut. Great. Now, I'm locked out of the house, with my talisman stuck inside. If I leave my house without my talisman, I'll be stuck as a cat until morning, but if I change back into a human to get back in, I run the risk of getting caught in the middle of a really embarrassing situation because I still haven't figured out how to keep my clothing during transformation. Mr. Brewer likes to enjoy his nighttime beverages on his front porch. I think he's being nosy, but Mom says he's probably just lonely. He meets my eye and shushes the terrier at his feet.

It's going to be a long night.

Mr. Brewer finally heads inside for the evening, and I seize the opportunity. I shimmy up my tree and balance across a thick branch near my window. I can feel the silent thrum of power from my talisman. I'm close enough to change here. Good. While it certainly would have been easier to walk back in through my front door, I ran the risk of running into Mom before I could reach the safety of my room and basketball shorts. Luckily, I'm able to transform back into human form and pull the window open. It's not as open as I would have liked, but it will have to do. I scrape and bang more body parts than I'd like to admit, but I'm back in my room and stumbling into pajamas when Mom storms back in.

"Mom! Sheesh, you could knock!"

"Knock? You're lucky you have a door!" Mom falls into a fit of frenzied yelling. She flips back and forth between English and Italian so quickly, I can scarcely keep up. Something about kidnappers coming back to finish her off and demon cats. I know better than to interrupt, and I wait it out with what I hope is interpreted as an apologetic expression. A quick glimpse at my nightstand clock says it is after nine o'clock.

"You can't do this, Felix. How many times before this gets through your thick skull?" She taps her index finger against my forehead. "Ay patatino. Your mother worries, you know. You can't just come and go whenever you please. I don't care what excuse you might have; nothing justifies this."

I'm glad Mom doesn't want to hear any lame excuse I could have come up with, and I wonder if she thinks I just lost track of time at Jay's house. Honestly at this point, I'm just grateful she hasn't murdered me. I'm still not sure what came over me. I've never seen a rat in the wild before, at least not as the cat. Is this the sort of reaction I can expect all the time? And what was that thing doing in my room? On my bed?

"That's why tomorrow you're coming with me to work at the store. A day of inventory will remind you the importance of responsibility."

Inventory? This is so unfair! It's not like I wanted to spend half the night listening to Mr. Brewer talk to his mom about her hemorrhoids. Now I won't get a chance to tell Jay about my dream or anything that just happened until we're at school.

I can't believe I'm saying this, but I hope Sunday speeds by. I can't wait for Monday.

Chapter Seven

Rainy Days Are the Worst

Don't ever say to yourself, "Hey! I bet it's fun to work at a girls accessory store." Because believe me, it's not. Sunday is absolute torture, and the only thing that's any good about it is Mom gets us drive-through on the way home.

Monday morning it rains. I hate the rain. Okay, I guess hate is a strong word, but I really don't like the rain. I don't like the way it makes the grass smell. I hate the drops of water spiking on my eyelashes, I hate the puddles that somehow always manage to ruin my good jeans. And I hate wet socks.

I also hate waiting in the rain. I'm tempted to start banging on Jay's window when he finally appears in his driveway. He gives me a frantic wave, and I know he must be wondering what I got in trouble for. He stopped by yesterday while I was still finishing up my burger and fries, but Mom turned him away at the door. I watch him talk to his mom for a moment, and then he opens his umbrella and wheels his bike toward me.

"Morning." I wish I thought to grab a hat or something. This rain is ridiculous. "Let's get going. I'll tell you why I'm grounded once we get there." I straddle my bike, but he doesn't move and remains huddled under his umbrella.

"We have to wait for Hunter."

If he told me we were waiting for Ethan, I would be less surprised. "Why? Why would you invite him?"

At least Jay looks embarrassed. "I didn't. I mean, not exactly. It just sort of came up yesterday, and I couldn't tell him no."

"Yesterday?" I can't hear anything else he is saying. "You hung out with him yesterday? You said you were going to be at Jackie's recital all day."

"I was! And then afterward I came over, like I said I would! Your mom said you were grounded, and I ran into Hunter on my way home. He asked if he could come over. What was I supposed to say?"

Umm, I don't know, maybe don't hang out with my enemy? I couldn't say that though. Jay would look at me even weirder than he is now. I can't blame him. There's no reason not to like Hunter.

I just don't.

Hunter's garage opens before I gather the courage to beg Jay not to invite him. He waves and wheels his bike toward us. He's wearing a Yankees ball cap and a dark-blue rain jacket. Great, another boy scout.

I roll my eyes, but neither of the guys seems to notice. Hunter mumbles something and Jay laughs. I clench my teeth before I say something I regret, but something comes out anyway.

"I thought you lived in Boston. Liar." I need to work on keeping my mouth shut.

Hunter's smile fades. "I, I did."

"But you're wearing a Yankees hat." No self-respecting Red Sox fan would ever be caught dead in Yankees gear. "You can't be a Boston fan wearing a Yankees hat."

"People can live in states different than their teams." Hunter looks like he's trying to hold in laughter.

"Yeah Felix, let it go. We're having a good morning."

I raise my eyebrows and look around. In the distance there's a crack of thunder. We are certainly not having a good morning.

"Boys! Let me drive you." Dr. Kim gestures for us all to enter her garage. She doesn't have to tell me twice. I'm soaked to the point that I'm sure I resemble a wet rat.

"You shouldn't be riding out in this. Jay, you know better." She mutters a few quiet words to him, and he nods back with an impatient bob to his toes. She ruffles his hair and tsks in my direction, mumbling as she gets in the car. I hear the words "umbrella" and "poor mother" before the car engine roars to a start.

I slide my kickstand up and leave my bike in the corner of the garage.

"Boys! We'll be late." Dr. Kim rolls down her window and gestures for us to hurry.

"Told you she'd make us ride with her," Jay says.

He and Hunter laugh. I wonder when he'd said that. Yesterday while they were hanging out? Had they checked the weather app together or something?

"Jay!" Dr. Kim's tone has lost all patience and my friend pales.

"I'm not riding up front with that. One of you will have to take one for the team." Jay chuckles as he reaches for the handle to open the door to the back seat of the sedan.

"Well I get car sick in the front. Sorry, Felix." Hunter does look sorry, but there is something about the nervous flutter of his fingers as they adjust his backpack that makes me want to slap the bag right off of him.

No! Nope, definitely no. I am so over this guy coming out of nowhere and messing up my life. I'm tired of his inside jokes with my best friend, and I'm not about to drive to school in the front seat of my pediatrician's car. It isn't fair! Jay is my best friend. I mean who even is this guy? There's an incessant pressure on my shoulder, almost like a persistent tap that grows stronger the more upset I get. Am I having a panic attack?

"Umm, Felix." I vaguely hear Jay's voice muffled against

 my ear. So close, so loud. At least Jay is paying attention to me now. I hope Hunter takes note. Jay is mine.

"Felix."

The tapping continues.

"Felix, stop bro!"

I blink, and suddenly I'm aware of just how close to Jay I am. We are shoulder to shoulder, and my head is cradled against his neck. What the—I jerk back so quickly, my book bag is flung off my shoulder. It falls to the ground.

"We're coming, Umma." Jay gestures to the back seat with a flourish.

Hunter climbs in quicker than I can blink. I stoop down and grab my bag. I feel like I'm slogging through honey.

Jay opens the passenger door. "I'll ride up front."

And leave me in the back with him? No thanks.

"No, I want to ride up with Dr. Kim." I try to charm her with my most winning smile, but she is so annoyed from waiting on us . . . well, me . . . that she isn't having it.

"Just get in the car," she shouts, and within seconds we are all buckled in, and she is pulling out of the drive.

"Hey, are you okay?" Jay leans forward to speak against my headrest. I know he's trying to whisper when he adds, "Was it something to do with . . . you know?"

Did he just make a hissing noise?

"I'm fine, Jay." I don't bother whispering my reply, but Hunter is playing with his cell phone—lucky!—and Dr. Kim has decided to ignore us in favor of some podcast on infantile probiotics, so it doesn't seem to matter.

The drive to school is short and silent. Halfway there it stops raining.

I am fine . . . aren't I? That's twice now that I've lost control of my body. It was like my brain left my body or something. I don't like it. It's Monday so I have plans to go to Miss Gray's after school anyway, but now, with everything going on, I'm actually in need of her wisdom. She'll know what all this means, and she can help with the Hunter problem. I just have to survive one day of school. Everything is going to be fine.

"I'm fine," I whisper.

Chapter Eight

Hunter, Hunter

Hunter has to check in at the principal's office. This is literally the best thing that's happened all morning. I wave a gleeful farewell as he leaves Jay and me standing in the main hallway. We aren't exactly late, but we have less than five minutes before the late bell. I can already see the anxiety clouding Jay's expression, but I have to talk to him.

"Jay, I—"

"What is going on with you?" Jay crosses his arms over his chest and gives me a careful once-over, like he's a teacher waiting for me to convince him that I don't need detention.

Everything rushes out: my weird dream, my suspicions about Hunter, and, what frightens me most, my loss of control over my powers.

"Is that what happened earlier? In the garage?" Now he just looks concerned. Super concerned, like I've just announced I'm dying of an incurable disease.

"Yeah, I guess so." I shrug, suddenly feeling awkward. "I mean, I think so. I just felt weird, like I might have a panic attack or something. Next thing I know, I'm giving you a bear hug."

"A bear hug?" Jay shakes his head and snorts out a tiny laugh. "Felix, you were like . . . nuzzling me. You rubbed your cheek all over my arm and shoulder, and that's not even the worst part."

It's not?

"At the end, once you'd snuggled up real close, you started purring."

"What?!" This definitely isn't a good development. Please be a one-time thing.

"And I think Hunter heard."

Oh no.

The bell rings before I can reply, and Jay gives me a pained look. "I'm sorry, but we'll talk later, okay? Just try to take it easy, okay buddy? We'll figure out what's wrong with you."

He jogs off for homeroom, leaving me to blink after him. What is wrong with me? Is Hunter really some creep out to get me, or is there something else behind all this? Is there something wrong with me?

I'm late for homeroom, but I can't seem to care. Everyone turns to look as I enter the room, and Mr. Hammond demands to

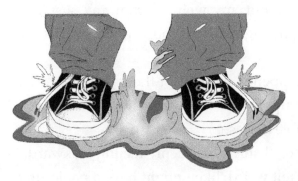

know why I'm tardy. I don't think I answer him, although, I may have muttered something about wet socks because a few of the kids giggled.

I take my seat next to Mckenna and struggle to bring the whiteboard in focus. Normally I would be trying to come up with something cool to say to Mckenna, but I'm too distracted to do anything more than feel sorry for myself. Mr. Hammond seems to notice I'm out of it too. He picks on me and makes me read the morning announcements as well as stand up to pass out the permission slips for the upcoming field day. Normally, the idea of field day would be exciting. All of the grades compete against one another, and the entire class gets the opportunity to represent their grade in their chosen sport. I'm running in the sixth-grade relay, but this morning my feet drag, and I can't picture myself running anything.

When the bell rings, I'm one of the last to gather my things and head toward the door.

I have language arts first period, which is as far from my homeroom as physically possible, but my feet just can't seem to move fast enough. My mind, though, is still racing. I should have paid more attention to Miss Gray's big lecture on hunters. I wonder if they are somehow able to mess with my powers, and that's why the cat has been acting strange. I try to think about the most recent mishap, rubbing my cheek on Jay. I remember seeing a video on YouTube that explained that cats have scent glands near their mouths, and they rub their cheeks to mark their territory. Was that what I was doing? Was I marking Jay? Claiming him as mine? Yet another unfair and bizarre side effect of being a werecat. I'd rather pee on him. It might have been less embarrassing.

I'm lost in thought and shuffling through the door when I

run into Mckenna.

Literally. She's standing her ground, blocking the doorway. "Oh, sorry, Mckenna."

"Are you?"

"Umm, yes?" There's something in her tone that makes me think she might be more than just a little mad at me. I try to remember if I've done anything to make her mad. Maybe I did something really dumb earlier and didn't know it too?

"What did you do this weekend? Stay busy?"

"Yeah, kinda." She raises her eyebrows, and I think she might be waiting for me to elaborate. But what can I say? I spent Saturday training as the cat and Sunday playing with ribbons? Vague silence is the better option.

Except I am certain that I've done the wrong thing.

"Fine," she says. "I guess I'll see you tomorrow morning."

"Well, and gym class and track practice later." What is her problem?

She whirls back around so quickly, her ponytail whips her in the face. It would have been funny if she wasn't so terrifying.

"Well, that's only if you're not too busy, right?"

"Huh? Not too busy? I have to go to class. Wha—"

She makes a sound of disgust and leaves me staring after her. What did I say wrong?

Midway through math class, I remember that I told Mckenna I would call her on Saturday. Last Friday, after track practice, Mckenna mentioned playing laser tag with her cousins, and I promised to call the next day to make plans. Only I had gotten so distracted with Hunter and the cat that I never did. Just great. No wonder Mckenna is so angry with me. Is it possible to get dumped by someone before they even become your girlfriend? Do I even want a girlfriend? I'm not sure I need the distraction. Between my major goof up with Mckenna and my problems with Hunter, I can safely say the rest of math class is a waste of time.

Social studies is my last class before lunch, and I'm gearing up for it to be another snooze fest, except that as soon as I enter the classroom, something is off. It's that smell again, the same one that made me go crazy yesterday. The smell that made me feel angry and wild. I clench my teeth and take short, gasping breaths through my mouth. Stay in control, Felix.

I know what I will find when I look toward the desks in the far corner of the room. The origin of the stench and the cause of my madness.

Hunter.

Here in my class, sitting in the seat next to the one assigned to me.

Of course.

I know with certainty that something is very wrong with Hunter. He watches me approach him, shoulders hunched together, chin lowered. He's removed the baseball cap of course—yay student dress code—and his hair is a rumpled mess.

He smiles at me. I scowl back.

"Let me guess, that's your desk." He juts his chin out toward the empty spot beside him.

I plop down into the chair by way of answer.

"Awesome." He sighs. "Look, I know why you don't . . ." He looks away and begins fidgeting with a pencil, spinning it nimbly between his fingers. The movement is quick and fluid and mesmerizing, and I can stare at nothing else. He seems to be battling with how to phrase something, but I can't imagine what he has to say to me.

I resist the urge to shake my head to clear it and instead take another deep breath. At least his smell seems to have died down somewhat.

"I just want to say that I know why you don't like me."

Fat chance. I don't even know why.

"I know that . . ." Once again he trails off, seemingly searching for the right words. Another big sigh. "Look, I can't imagine what it must feel like having . . . well, someone like me suddenly showing up on your turf. But I don't want to fight, okay? And my family doesn't want any trouble either." He clenches his fist, and the pencil snaps. "Our kind doesn't have to be enemies."

I've been kicked in the stomach, or at least it feels that way.

I replay the words in my mind. Our kind doesn't have to be enemies . . . our kind. I've been right all along. Hunter and his entire family are dangerous.

He's a hunter.

Chapter Nine

I'd Like to Phone a Friend

I stare at him. If he's a hunter, then why hasn't he drained my magic and killed me? What does he mean, we don't have to be enemies? Because I can imagine it's pretty difficult to be someone's friend while they're attempting to murder you. Or is he somehow a good guy? No, I don't believe it. I'm still trying to figure it out when the bell rings to start class. Our moment to hash things out is over for now.

Miss Landers "surprises" us with a guest speaker and then stares at us from the back of the classroom, assuring no more questions even if I figured out what to ask. The lecture is excruciating, and about a billion years later, the bell rings again, and the students begin assembling their things. Hunter lingers, as if knowing I would have further questions for him. We walk out of the classroom together and begin talking over one another as soon as we're in the hallway.

"What did you mean we don't have to be enemies?"

"Can we talk later? Maybe after school?" His eyes dart back and forth, scanning the hall.

Of course Jay chooses this exact moment to arrive. He looks slightly out of breath like he must have run to get here. I wonder if he somehow knew Hunter and I had a class together. And then I wonder if Hunter asked him to meet him after class.

I narrow my eyes at his coincidental timing.

"Hey, Jay."

Hunter waves in that quick frantic movement of his and gives me a warning look as if to say, We'll talk about this later.

Jay gives us both a careful look. I try to smile at him, but my thoughts are racing. If Hunter isn't a hunter, then what did he mean when he said, "Our kind doesn't have to be enemies"? And why did he have this strange effect on me? I pat the baseball card in my pocket, always aware of the dim hum of power coming from it. I don't think it's my imagination. The card is getting hot. Is it because I'm too close to Hunter?

Hunter pulls out his cell phone and seems to be texting someone. He catches me watching him and quickly puts it away. "So, Felix was just saying lunch here is the worst?" Hunter raises his eyebrows at me, as though daring me to contradict him.

"Eh, the pizza's not so bad. Speaking of . . . y'all ready? I'm starving." I force a fake smile and keep my focus on my talisman in my pocket. I still feel in control of my powers, and I want to keep it that way.

"Pizza? I'm getting extra cheese." Hunter slings either arm over each of our shoulders, sandwiching himself between me and Jay.

He continues to chatter on about his day, and I allow myself to be pulled along, my thoughts a flurry of worries. What did Hunter mean? And how did he seem to know so much about everything? Miss Gray said I was hidden to Were hunters, but clearly Hunter and his family have a way of bypassing that. Could I really believe that he and his family don't want any trouble? That they won't be a threat to me? To Miss Gray? Ugh, this day can't end fast enough.

The three of us shuffle through the line, and each of us orders a pizza with milk. I try to catch Hunter's eye, but he has pasted a derpy smile on his face and seems to be actively avoiding eye contact. Fine.

I turn toward a semi-empty bench on the perimeter of the cafeteria. The three of us can fit if we throw out the small pile of garbage and discarded food trays. If we were a bit quicker through the line, we might have managed better seats.

Hunter ignores the bench and continues walking to the large share table in the center of the cafeteria. I mean, sure, there are a few empty seats, but the table is full of students already. Eighth graders mostly, with a handful of sixth graders deemed cool enough to sit among them. Ethan being one of them. We haven't had time to fill Hunter in on all our mortal enemies or he would have known there was no way Jay and I would attempt to sit at this table. No matter how much we may have wanted to.

I notice Mckenna sitting at the far end. She's in deep discussion with an older girl, her sister, I think, and doesn't notice me staring. That's another problem I'm going to have to fix. I can't believe I forgot to call her after I promised I would. That's, like, girl rule number one.

"Right, Felix?" Jay elbows me, giving me an anguished look.

Oops, I haven't been paying attention. Luckily, Jay repeats himself.

"We can't exactly just go and sit anywhere. I mean, you're new so you can try to make friends with . . ." Jay trails off as Hunter ignores him and continues toward the table.

Hunter simply sets his tray down at the end and smiles down the length of the table. "Hi, we'd like to sit here. Umm, could y'all squish down a bit?"

Ethan turns away from his conversation with Lenny and meets Hunter's eyes. Then he looks over at Hunter's tray, at his single slice of pizza and fifteen packets of parmesan cheese, and then back up at Hunter. Hunter raises his eyebrows, and somehow his smile grows even wider.

Ethan stands up with a shrug. "I was just leaving anyway. See you in gym, Triple F." He shoulders me as he walks by, but for the most part, that was the tamest reaction I've had from him all year. And after we stole his seats too. Soon there is a shuffling of feet as everyone makes room and slides down the bench.

Hunter takes his seat and begins pouring cheese over his pizza.

I wouldn't believe it if I hadn't been watching it all happen in slow motion in front of me. Some weird hunter powers? Possibly. It doesn't make sense. Miss Gray said they didn't have any magic of their own.

I guess I'm not the only one impressed because Jay lets out a whistle.

"I don't know how you got Ethan to do that, but it was incredible." He plops down next to Hunter, leaving me to take the empty seat across from him.

"Yeah," I agree. "How did you do it? Some kind of magic?" I can't help but ask.

Hunter laughs. "No magic, just nepotism."

"Nepa-what?"

"Means he knows Ethan before or —"

"He's my cousin," Hunter supplies. "Only through marriage," he rushes on. He must have seen the shock on our faces. "His family is pretty distant from mine. But they're how my family came to know about this town." It takes a moment for that to sink in. Is that why I don't like him? Do my cat senses somehow know he is related to my enemy? I doubt it. Something is off with Hunter, I'm sure of it. And then he admitted it out loud to me.

I want to talk to Jay a bit more about everything, but Hunter is right next to him, and I'm not given an opportunity. Worse, Mckenna finally notices me from the other end of the table. She lifts her hand as though she is about to wave but then seems to think better of it. Her head dips back down toward her sister. Great.

I'm not even sure how much of my pizza I manage to eat. Between the death looks from Mckenna and the dodgy questions from Jay and Hunter, I'm not surprised by the oncoming headache.

I stand up, trying to shove my chair back from the shared table. I've forgotten I'm on a bench and I nearly fall back, barely managing to turn and catch myself at the last moment.

Jay frowns but doesn't say anything, probably trying not

to draw any more attention to me.

"Where are you going?" Hunter asks, cocking his head toward me.

Is it my imagination or is there a sinister glare behind his words?

"Bathroom break?" He snorts at his joke and empties an entire packet of parmesan cheese into his mouth. Gross.

"I just remembered, I need to get to my next class early."

"Gym?" Jay's eyebrows knit together. He's still frowning. Too late, I see him realize what I was trying to do, and he lowers his head. "Sorry," he mutters so softly that, if I didn't have cat hearing, I wouldn't have heard it.

"Uh, bathroom break because I need to change shorts before gym class because — " I cut myself off, realizing how gross this excuse is starting to sound. "Okay, see you then." The words run together, and I scurry away before I can make an even bigger idiot out of myself.

My talisman burns a hole in my pocket, and my skin is hot and tingly. I take a deep breath, for once grateful for the school's open hallways. It's always super hot or freezing cold, but right now I gulp down the fresh air like a drowning man. Great, another panic attack. What is Hunter doing to me?

I can't wait to speak to Miss Gray another moment. I need a plan.

It is easy to convince the nurse to let me use her office telephone to call home and request allergy medicine from my mom. She doesn't even bother to confirm whether I'm actually calling my mom or whether I actually have allergies. The phone is ancient, the kind you see on those old TV shows. It has tons of extra buttons, and a long, curly cord connects the earpiece. Miss Gray answers after the second ring.

"Hello! It's me." I am so relieved she answers, it doesn't even occur to me that she might not know who I am.

"Felix? Are you in some sort of trouble?"

I look over at the nurse, but she seems to be ignoring me for the most part. I stretch as far as the phone cord will go and mumble into the receiver.

"I am. We all are. There's a family of hunters that moved to our street. One of them is with me at school and . . ." I take a deep breath, preparing myself for her howl of anger. "He knows my secret."

"Impossible. As I informed you earlier, Weres are hidden until the light of a total lunar eclipse."

"But I'm sure of it! He knows," I hiss into the phone, and Nurse Kate looks up with concern. I give her a thumbs up and cup my hand around the receiver. "He knows what I am. I need to know what to do next."

The silence stretches for so long, I wonder if we have somehow gotten disconnected. "Umm, Miss Gray?"

"Leave immediately after school today. No

extracurriculars, no athletics. Come straight in. Don't stand on ceremony waiting for me to answer the door. I hope you're wrong, Felix, because if you're not and you're suddenly visible to hunters . . . well, you and your mother can say goodbye to the life you used to know. I have to go now. There is much I must prepare for."

The phone clicks and falls into an obnoxious hum that takes me several seconds to register as a dial tone. Slowly, I replace the phone in its cradle. I thank the nurse and head off to change for gym class, though it's hard to imagine focusing on dodgeball when Miss Gray has basically warned me that Mom and I are in mortal danger.

Hunter is in the locker room. He gives me a thumbs up and asks if everything went smoothly. I ignore the question and focus on shoving my book bag into my locker. Ethan walks in after his cousin, but he gives him a wide berth. Maybe Ethan and I have something in common after all. He saunters over to me, his lips curled up in a sneer. Or maybe I'm getting ahead of myself.

"Yo, Triple F. You ready to eat my dust this afternoon?"

Oh no. I've completely forgotten. Today Ethan, Mckenna, and I are all set to race for the anchor position in our grade's relay team. I allowed Ethan to beat me a few weeks ago at a local meet, and I was looking forward to the opportunity to dish a little payback. If I miss the race, I won't have a chance at the anchor spot, but if I stay, not only can I secure my spot, but I might have a chance to smooth things over with Mckenna. The last thing I want is for her to hate me forever just because I can't pick up a stupid phone.

"Don't worry, I'll be there." Maybe I'm crazy for postponing Miss Gray, but I can't say no to a challenge. And besides, what's the worst that could happen?

Chapter Ten

Faint Forgiveness

Mckenna is late. She takes forever to show up to the empty field, and I begin to worry I've made a terrible mistake, wasting time like this. Even Ethan is annoyed. I hear him muttering about how girls always take forever to get ready.

The two of us stand on the field, not bothering to look at one another. We had an uneasy truce, but it seems like lately he's been falling into old habits. That's why I surprise myself when I start talking.

"So, must be nice having your cousin move to town."

His head jerks up toward me, and his eyes widen just slightly before he shakes his head and turns his attention back to his shoelaces. "If you say so."

"Are you guys close?"

"No."

Well, this is pointless.

"He's weird," he mutters. "Him and his family, they're just some people we send Christmas cards to." He looks uncomfortable with the conversation, but I don't want to let it drop.

"Weird how? Do they—"

"Hey guys! Sorry." Mckenna jogs up and offers us both an apologetic smile. "I had to convince Miley to wait for me." She waves back at her sister, who stands several feet away with a pained look on her face.

"It's okay, we barely noticed." Ethan smiles at her, and I roll my eyes. Right, I guess we're pretending that he wasn't just complaining about how girls always take three times as long as guys.

At this point I'm finding it hard to break my focus from my problems with Hunter. Just a quick race and then I can hurry to Miss Gray for answers. Tomorrow everything will be better.

I try not to make the race look too easy, but there's no way I'm letting Ethan beat me. The three of us cross the finish marker mere seconds apart, but I'm in the lead and Ethan is in last. Mckenna is getting faster. She would definitely beat me if I didn't have superpowers.

Ethan leaves in a hurry, and I should do the same. I honestly should have left an hour ago, but I linger because this is my chance to make things right with Mckenna.

"Is your mom coming to pick you guys up?" I nod toward Miley, who tosses her hands up in an impatient gesture. Mckenna holds out a finger and takes a deep breath. She looks like she is on the verge of tears. She shakes her head just slightly and clenches and unclenches her fist. I notice a tick in her jaw. She takes another deep breath before she punches me on the arm.

"Seriously, Felix?"

Ouch! I won't admit it to Jay, but that was the hardest hit I've ever taken.

"I know, about Saturday . . ." What do I say? Obviously not the truth, but what lie can possibly justify not calling after I promised I would? What a time for my mind to go blank!

"Ugh. Just forget it, Felix. I have to talk to Fitz before we leave. And no, our mom isn't coming to pick us up." She turns and begins walking toward her sister. I have to dig from my cat speed reserve to catch up with her.

"Wait, please. Just two minutes." I grab her arm to stop her. Intense heat shoots up through my fingers, and a jolt of electricity runs down the length of my arm. I immediately release her, but it's too late. A series of images flash through my mind. I can't explain them all—some are clear, movie-like images of Mckenna and her family or memories of her and me. Some are abstract, a feeling of intense emotion, a particular smell. Then everything goes black.

"Felix! Felix, please, wake up!"

When I open my eyes, Mckenna's braces are the first thing I see. The metallic pink glows in the afternoon light.

"He's okay," Miley announces.

It takes me a moment to realize why I'm on the ground. I think I fainted. How embarrassing.

"Are you okay?" Mckenna kneels beside me, her sky-blue eyes filled with concern.

"I think so. I mean, yeah! I'm sorry. I didn't mean to scare you guys." I try to stand up, but the best I can do is to sit up with my legs bent under me. I think I might puke.

"Maybe you should go inside and see the nurse."

I accept her offered hand and finally stagger to my feet.

"No, I'm fine! I, uh— " I need to get to Miss Gray's. "I'm just gonna head home."

Miley shrugs and mutters something to Mckenna about important home ec homework before giving me a pointed look. "Get home safe. I'd feel bad if you, like, died on the way home or something."

Right. Thanks. I nod and toss up a hand in farewell, and Mckenna turns to give me one final look-over.

"Are you sure you're all right? If you need a friend, I'm here, okay?"

"Thank you. Seriously. And Mckenna?"

"Yeah?"

"I know this doesn't make any sense, but I really did have a good excuse for not calling you Saturday night. I'm sorry."

She smiles, and once again her braces catch the sunlight. "Felix, it's okay. I believe you." She waves once more before trotting off to join her sister. I watch the two of them walk down the street for a few moments before I suddenly remember my bike is still in Jay's garage. Great, just wonderful. Now I have to walk home.

I don't live far, but just far enough that the walk will be annoying. Not to mention that I'll be even later to meet with Miss Gray. I wonder if she'll be upset that I'm tardy. We typically meet on Mondays and Wednesdays, and lately most Friday evenings and Saturday mornings so long as Mom doesn't need me around at home. So far the training sessions are all very serious, and I only expect them to get worse. Especially after this weekend's warnings and Hunter's sudden appearance. That wasn't a coincidence, I'm sure of it. And then there were all these sudden power surges and now this blackout. There has to be a connection.

I make a mental checklist. If there's still time after my meeting with Miss Gray, I'll need to stop by Jay's to fill him in. I definitely don't want him to continue interacting with enemy number one. And that is going to be another problem, I realize with a big sigh. How am I supposed to ensure Jay's safety when he's literally living next door to someone so dangerous? My backpack is heavy on my shoulders, and I shift it to gain more comfort.

The longer I walk, the more I begin to realize what a dumb thing I'd just done. I should have gone straight home, straight to Miss Gray. Was securing the anchor position in the relay race really so important? It seemed so at the time, but now I'm not so sure. I'm just cresting the hill to our cul-de-sac when I remember Mom is going to be home early today. If she's not home already. She knows I'm expected at Miss Gray's, but if, for some reason, she sees my bike at Jay's or realizes I'm not with Miss Gray, I'll be grounded for eternity. I break into a jog, even tapping into the cat for a boost of extra speed.

It's been a long day, and I think the absolute worst way to end it would be with a fight with Mom.

I'm wrong.

I smell Hunter before I see him, and his stench pulls me to

a halt. He doesn't seem to notice me as he pedals his bike toward his house. Is he coming from Miss Gray's? It's difficult to say, but there's little else in the cul-de-sac. It's possible he's just riding around, but there have been too many coincidences lately. Why would Hunter go to Miss Gray?

I'm breathing hard by the time I walk up the gravel drive. I'm tired from sprinting almost half the way, but I'm eager to get some answers, and I still want to talk to Jay before I'm expected home. I swing open the front door to Miss Gray's home, and I'm greeted by the usual odors of dried flowers, peppermint, and tuna.

"Miss Gray?" I call out as I step inside.

I'm suddenly reminded of the first time I entered her home without knocking. The time that cursed me with the cat. The best and yet also the worst thing that ever happened to me.

"Miss Gray?" I call out again, and this time it is hard to ignore the rapid sinking feeling in my stomach.

She wouldn't have left anywhere. She wouldn't. Not after she told me to go directly to her house after school.

But if Miss Gray isn't here, then where is she?

I give the house a careful once-over before I'm convinced Miss Gray truly isn't home.

It's weird, and this fact mixed in with the rest of the events from today doesn't sit well with me. She wouldn't have left without a note. And then I notice the most frightening detail of all. Miss Gray's book is sitting out on her dining room table. She said she would never do that. I am certain now that something awful happened to her. Did the hunters get to her first? Did Hunter get to her?

The familiar sound of Mom's Range Rover on our driveway pricks my ears and signifies that if I value my freedom, I need to get home immediately. I tell myself Miss Gray will pop up later this evening or tomorrow morning with lectures and assignments on being the cat.

I hope I'm right.

I open the front door to Miss Gray's house and struggle for a moment over whether I should lock it or not. I don't want Miss Gray's house to be vulnerable to robbers, but I also don't want to lock Miss Gray out if she intentionally left her house this way. I settle for locking the front and sneaking out the back, weaving along the fence line toward home. With any luck I can sneak back home and inside my room before Mom even notices my missing bike.

Getting back inside before Mom is one of the easiest things I've done today. I'm sitting at the table pretending to do homework when she walks in. She smiles when she sees me, and for a brief moment, I can pretend that everything is fine, and there isn't a family of dangerous hunters living across the street.

Chapter Eleven

Rat in the Maze

I'm having another weird dream. Once again I'm aware that I'm dreaming, and once more I am in the maze stuck in between some extra-cool version of myself and the cat. I walk down a long hallway. White light illuminates just how bare and boring the hallway is, but I can't find the light source, and I know in the back of my mind that something is dangerous about this place.

Distant laughter reaches my ears, and I try to ignore the goosebumps that prickle up my arms. It's just a dream, I remind myself.

"Felix."

The disembodied voice comes from everywhere and nowhere all at once, an invisible surround sound that somehow erupts in my head as well.

"Felix, you must find me."

"Miss Gray?" It doesn't sound like her, but then the voice doesn't really sound like anybody. My only response is more laughter, so my only choice is to keep walking forward. After walking for at least an hour or seven — who knows how slow time moves in the dream world — the hall comes to a stop, forking off in either direction. One way is another hallway, identical to the one I'm in. The other hallway is the same except for one noticeable difference. That smell. Hunter. I turn right and follow my nose. Why is Hunter in my dream? Is that the voice I heard? Is this all just a trap? I look down at my hand, flexing my fingers and contracting my claws. If it is, I'll be ready. The smell grows stronger as I continue down the hall.

"Hunter?" More laughter. "Quit playing games." There is

no mistaking that smell, but Hunter is nowhere to be found. The smell is so strong, I should practically be on top of the guy, but the hallway remains empty.

No, not empty. There, just ahead of me, is a tiny, spotted rat.

The creature seems to notice me at the same time because it squeaks and stands up on its hind legs. The rat has white fur with brown spots. Its whiskers wriggle, and its nose twitches as it smells the air between us. The rat examines me for a moment, tilting its head to one side and peering at me with its dark, beady eyes.

Then the rat begins to laugh.

Rats can laugh? The dim thought pierces my foggy brain. What is the meaning of this dream?

"Felix. Come to me." That same voice, definitely not

coming from the rat, settles over me. The rat stops laughing, apparently listening to the same voice.

"Felix!" The voice is more determined, screaming in my head so loudly, it rattles my brain and I fall to my knees.

The rat scampers toward me, stopping just inches from my clenched hands.

"Felix," the rat says. "Run."

My eyes snap open, and Mom is suddenly in focus, her brown eyes wide with concern. "Patatino." She tsks softly. "Are you all right, my love? You were screaming. You must have had a bad dream."

"I'm fine," I breathe out more shakily than I want to admit. "Hey, Mom, can rats laugh?"

Her eyebrows knit together, and she presses her palm against my forehead. "Gross, I hope not. What makes you ask?" She looks around the room suspiciously, probably looking for any traces of more rats.

"Nothing. Forget it." I push up to a sitting position and squint at the sunlight filtering in through my blinds.

She frowns, but her gaze follows mine and then she nods. "Yup, it was almost time for you to wake up anyway. Why don't you get dressed, and I'll make us both some pancakes." She cups my face with her hand before leaving, and it's not until after she's shut the door that I feel I can truly shake off the lingering effects of my dream. What did it all mean?

I can think of nothing else the entire time I shower and brush my teeth, so it's little wonder that I'm powering up my laptop while searching for socks. Finally I find a matching pair without any holes, and I'm typing "can rats laugh" into my search engine.

Q can rats laugh?   ✕

They can. Apparently, it's done in a frequency most humans can't hear. That doesn't make me feel better.

Neither do Mom's pancakes, and they always do the trick. I can tell I'm doing a bad job of hiding my anxiety when she offers to stay home and watch movies with me. Sheesh, I must look pathetic.

"I'm fine, Mom. I need to get to school. Um, important math thing." I don't even have the energy to come up with a good lie. Lucky for me, Mom doesn't press it and tells me to use the nurse's office if I need to. I can't tell her that I used that trick up yesterday so I just nod weakly and hug her goodbye. Which probably only worries her more.

"Are you sure everything is okay? Do you want to talk about your nightmare?" She pauses. "Do you want to call your father?"

"No. I'm okay, really. I promise." I really am worrying her if she's offering to call Dad. The two of them don't get along at all. I can't blame her, not after the way he suddenly announced he had to move away without any explanation. But I can't think about all that now. "I really should go."

"I love you, Felix."

"Love you too." Sheesh, are we done yet? I practically run out of the house before Mom can bust out the baby pictures.

My bike is still in Jay's garage, so I hurry across the street and am about to knock on his front door when it opens. Jackie, Jay's older sister, blinks down at me.

"Oh, hello. Why are y'all up so early? Never mind, I don't care. They're in his room." She places earbuds in either ear and jogs out the door for her morning run. It's not until after I close the door behind her that I register what she said. They're in his room? Who is? But I have a sinking suspicion I know the answer.

Jay and Hunter are both peering down at a piece of curved glass. They look up when I enter. Jay smiles and Hunter waves. Like everything is normal. I bite the inside of my cheek to keep myself from groaning out loud. So much for telling Jay about my dream.

"Hey, Felix. What are you doing here?"

Jay sets down the plastic telescope part and walks toward me. I know it's just an expression, but I hate that Hunter has enough audacity to question what I'm doing at my best friend's house. I realize I've started making a low growling sound in the back of my throat, and I cut it off with a nervous cough.

"I was just showing Hunter my lab setup. He's entering the STEM fair too." Jay's tone is slightly defensive, probably because he's been caught with public enemy number one, but at the moment, I have more important things to worry about.

"Jay, we need to talk." I give Hunter a pointed glare. "Alone."

Hunter sets down the last of Jay's project and heads for the door. His shoulder brushes mine as he leaves, and once again, I'm hit with his smell. He stops in the doorway, and I'm forced to hold my breath. How is it that he and the rat from my dream have the same odor? What does it mean?

"Um, Jay? My bike is still in your garage."

"It's okay. We'll be down in just a minute," Jay replies with a dismissive wave.

"Actually, we might be a while. We have a lot to talk about." I drop my book bag between my feet on Jay's carpet and raise my eyebrows at Hunter, daring him to disagree.

Jay begins to protest, but Hunter cuts him off. "It's fine. I should get going anyway. See you guys in class later." He waves, and Jay and I wait until we hear the garage door close before we start speaking.

"Please tell me this isn't about Hunter and his family being hunters." I've seen this expression on Jay once before. Last time, it was right after Samantha Teaks vomited right in front of him. Her puke was cotton candy pink.

"You won't be saying that after you hear what I have to tell you." I fill Jay in on the details of yesterday's afternoon and last night's dream. His eyes widen as my story spills out.

"So what are you going to do now? You can't just keep waiting around for another blackout."

"I don't have to. I'm going to confront Hunter about everything. He's already opened up and said that we don't have

72

to be enemies. Maybe he means that. I mean, we don't know for sure that he's doing any of this on purpose. Maybe hunters just have this weird effect on Weres."

"Yeah, maybe." Jay doesn't sound so convinced. "What does Miss Gray think about this?"

"Well, I didn't actually get to talk to her yesterday. She wasn't home when I got there." I suddenly remember seeing Hunter by her house and ask Jay if he thinks they know each other.

He shrugs. "I'm not sure, Felix. I don't think Hunter is dangerous, bu—"

"He is!" I insist.

"But if he is, then you need to be careful. Just don't do anything stupid. At least, not until you talk to Miss Gray about it."

We leave for school shortly after, and I plan out my confrontation with Hunter along the way. It wasn't that long ago that I planned an act of revenge on Ethan, the class bully. And I thought I had problems then.

Jay and I make it to our homerooms just in time. Mckenna smiles brightly as I take my seat next to her. "Hey, Woolfe, you feeling better?" Her blue eyes sparkle, even under the stupid fluorescent lights.

"Yeah, definitely." I fix a big smile on my face and focus on not saying anything stupid. I'm just lucky that I did faint yesterday, otherwise, how would I have gotten her to forgive me?

"That's good." She looks like she wants to ask something else, but Mr. Hammond begins taking attendance and saying the morning announcements, so I allow my thoughts to wander. I'm not sure when will be the best time to confront Hunter. He seemed to be open to talking, so long as it was done in private. I guess my best bet is to get him cornered and by himself after school. That way I'll get to talk to Miss Gray, hopefully, and get an actual plan in place. Then, once he admits what he is, I'll be able to make him stop the blackouts . . . so long as he's the one behind them.

Mr. Hammond announces that we can utilize the rest of the period as free time, and Mckenna turns to me expectantly.

"Do you think Ethan is mad we beat him?"

Yesterday's race seems like a million years ago, but I'm glad she brought it up. Representing our grade is a big deal, and Fitz picked the three of us personally. We are the fastest kids in our class, but my speed might have just a teeny tiny cat booster. I try not to use my abilities when competing, but sometimes, at least when it concerns Ethan, I let him bring out the competitive side in me.

"He'll get over it. Who do you think Fitz will place as our fourth? Ellie?"

The noise level in the classroom escalates as more students take advantage of their free time. Mckenna leans over her desk toward me. I could hear her fine, but I don't mind. "No, Ellie is out." She rolls her eyes. "With a broken finger. She said it hurts to hold the baton. Drama queen. Anyway, Fitz said she has someone in mind. They're running today if you want to stop by and watch. Fitz says they might be a good prospect for the team too. Really, you should go and report back to me who it is. I can't be there because we're going to the shelter after school."

"The shelter?"

"The animal shelter. Mom's letting me get my own cat! Hey, did Jay ever find his?"

The bell rings, saving me from any answer. I'd rather not explain to her that I'm sometimes a cat owned by my best friend.

I manage to catch a quick catnap during language arts, so I am refreshed for math class. Good thing, too, since Mr. Jones throws a pop quiz on long division. This is just the first bad thing that happens. Leaving class, I step in gum that some jerk spit on the sidewalk. The gummy substance is bright green and smears across the white rubber band of my left sneaker. Awesome. Ethan bumps into me after. Literally. My backpack flies off my shoulder, and he makes a crack about how I should be fast enough to stay out of his way. I'd say he's mad we beat him.

I guess you could also say I'm in a less-than-perfect mood by the time I make it to social studies. Well, that's fine. I don't need to be in a good mood to sit next to Hunter. He seems to notice the moment I enter the room because his head whips up, and his eyes meet mine.

Remember, it's better to wait until after school and after a talk with Miss Gray. Don't confront him. Best to ignore him.

But Hunter doesn't make it easy. He leans toward me as soon as I take my seat.

"Hey, we need to talk."

No, not now. Should I ignore him? Tell him we need to do it later? I open my mouth to tell him to shove off, but before I can say anything, my talisman buzzes in my pocket. I reach for it, too late realizing how hot it is to the touch.

"Felix? Hey, you don't look so—hey! Felix! Help, someone!"

The last things I see are Hunter's beady brown eyes, magnified under his glasses.

Chapter Twelve

Late-Night Catventures

When I wake up, the first thing I feel is embarrassment. The entire class is huddled around me, talking over one another. I hear someone ask if I'm dead.

Mrs. Landers fans me with a stack of worksheets.

"Don't move, darling," she says in her Louisiana drawl. "Hunter ran to go get Nurse Kate."

Wonderful, I think. I know a trip to the nurse's office isn't necessary, but I'm not dumb enough to waste a get-out-of-class freebie. Nurse Kate arrives and helps me to her office where she makes me lie down with a cool compress while she calls my mom.

Apparently, fainting in the middle of class is enough to get you out of school for the rest of the day! The downside is that Mom is crazy worried when she comes to pick me up and takes me straight to Dr. Kim's office.

Dr. Kim's office is cool if you're a baby. The walls are painted in brightly colored murals, and there are huge tubs of building blocks in the waiting room. Luckily, we are shown to a room nearly right away.

I allow my mind to wander as Mom and Dr. Kim make small talk and Mom describes my "symptoms," which is especially difficult considering I don't really have any. After she takes a blood sample, Dr. Kim runs through a list of questions, some of them embarrassing like when was the last time I pooped. Seriously? I swear that I'm fine. I even try to convince them I just fell asleep. Finally, Dr. Kim announces that I am healthy and attributes my growth spurt and low blood sugar to my sleepless night and blackout. She gives Mom a referral to a few specialists just in case. It's late in the afternoon by the time we make it back home, and I look with some longing at Jay's bike left out on his porch. He's home.

"Mom, can I go over to Jay's house?" I ask the question as a formality, but Mom firmly shakes her head.

"No, absolutely not. Felix, you were unconscious at school today!" Her cell phone rings, but she ignores the call and slams the phone on the table.

"For, like, a second." I scratch at my neck, uncomfortable with this conversation. "I'm fine."

"We don't know that. I don't . . . Son, if this happens again, it could mean something serious."

Good thing I didn't mention yesterday.

"I want you to go upstairs to your room and just relax. Read a book or something, okay?" Her phone rings again, and she scowls down at it. "I have to take this. Afterward I'll make you up some chicken orzo, hmm? Go upstairs. Rest."

I go upstairs and shut the door to my room. I want to fill Jay in on what happened. And I still need to talk to Miss Gray. I'm pushing my luck, but I need answers more. I take my talisman out of my pocket and attach it to the cat collar I keep shoved beneath my mattress, and then I turn into the cat. It's not as painful an experience as it once was, and I think my body is growing used to it. It always starts with the tiny black hairs that grow rapidly across my body. Long claws retract from beneath my finger beds, and fangs grow from my teeth. My body both lengthens and shrinks, contorting until I am no longer human.

The thing I miss most when I'm the cat? Thumbs. Too late I realize that I can't put my collar on myself, and it's too small to fit as a human. I scoop up the baseball card and clamp it between my teeth. I'll just have to carry it until I can get someone to attach it. I jump from my carpet to my desk chair to the windowsill in seconds. Luckily, I remembered to leave the window open so at least I'm saving time there. Now, if I can just manage to handle my business and get back inside before Mom catches me . . .

It's early in the evening, so I have to be especially careful of traffic. I pick my way down the street, staying close to people's yards and keeping a careful watch for evening dog-walkers. Miss Gray's house is ominous, blocking the early evening sun and casting dark shadows into the street. Maybe she's inside. But even as I have the thought, I don't feel optimistic.

I sneak around to the back yard so I can go in through the kitchen. Not that it was left open or anything, but I feel like neighbors are less likely to notice a naked kid breaking into the house if it's happening in the back yard.

I can tell as soon as I open the door that she hasn't returned home. I change back into the cat to see if there is anything I might have missed with my human eyes, but there is nothing of note except the exposed grimoire. I eye it nervously but leave it on the table. If cats could sigh, I would do so now. Miss Gray isn't here, and there are no new clues. Except . . . I lift my nose to the air,

sniffing around. I was right. There is another smell aside from Miss Gray. One that has become annoyingly familiar. Hunter.

I know where she is. That's it. I need to talk to Jay now. I don't know how, but I'm getting Miss Gray back from Hunter and his family tonight.

I race across the street and to the safety of Jay's yard. His garage is open wide, and pop music blares from a tiny pink speaker. Jackie sings and dances along to the beat as she washes her Civic. The car is older than she is, but she cleans it, like, every weekend. Technically, I still owe her a few car washes, but it's best not to remind people about these sorts of things. Anyway, the open garage is the perfect entry point for a cat trying to sneak into a house. I run past Jackie while she's distracted and "oooo ohhhhing" about some heartbreak and enter the house without anyone spotting me. I don't have any time to waste, so I hurry through the kitchen and down the hall leading to Jay's bedroom.

I hear voices at the same time that the stench of Hunter washes over me.

Hunter shushes Jay, and the voices stop. I freeze in the hallway, certain that Hunter is aware of my presence just as I'm aware of his. Seconds later, Jay enters the hallway, stopping short once he sees me.

"It's okay," he calls out. "It's just my cat." His eyes widen as they return to mine.

"You have a cat?" Hunter appears in Jay's doorway. He frowns at me.

"Uh, yeah. He's, uh, kind of a free spirit." Jay gives me a look that screams, What are you doing? "Are you allergic?"

"No." Hunter keeps his distance, regarding me from afar. "Cats don't normally like me."

That's an understatement. I realize how ridiculous I must look, clutching a sparkly collar—Jay's idea of a joke—and a baseball card between my teeth. At least I'm not rubbing up against Jay's sneakers . . . yet. I wonder if Hunter truly believes I'm an innocent cat or if he knows exactly who I am. For a moment it seems like we will all be stuck in this hallway forever, but then Hunter slowly nods.

"You know, there's something I forgot I'm in charge of back at home. I better go and check on that."

I glare in his direction, resisting the urge to hiss. Yeah, I bet he has something or someone to check on. Hunter ducks back into the room to gather his things and then he leaves, giving me a wide berth. Jay and I watch him leave and then rush to his bedroom.

I transform in his closet. It's the safest option for privacy and offers me something to wear. When I come out, Jay sits on his bed, his face grim.

"Felix! How are you? Everyone at school was talking about how you fainted in class. Mckenna is, like, super worried. She gave me her number and made me swear that I would call her the moment we talked."

As amazing as that information is, I can't focus on it at the moment. I quickly tell Jay about my discovery at Miss Gray's house and my suspicions.

"I believe you," Jay interrupts me. "I believe it all. Felix, you should sit down." He gestures toward his gaming chair, and I sit on the edge, tapping my foot impatiently.

"What is it? Jay, just tell me."

"Hunter came by after school, as you know, but he didn't come here just to see me or anything. I think he came here looking for information on you. He said that he qualified with Fitz for some race, and he was worried you would hate him for that."

"Wait, back up. Hunter did what?" I won't say Miss Gray is forgotten, but I do make some room to process this new info. So Hunter is the mystery student Fitz found as our fourth in the relay. I can't believe I'm so unlucky. Why is this guy involving himself in my entire life? "He has to be stopped. I'm not racing with him!"

"Hang on," Jay says. He begins pacing in front of me. "That's not even what you should be focusing on."

"But he—"

"Felix! I think he only told me about the race as some lame

82

excuse to start asking me all these questions about you. He said it was so he could try to forge a friendship with you. He wants you to be good teammates, and at first, I thought, oh that's nice. But then the questions were weird. Like, how long had you been racing and if you were record-breaking fast. And how many pets you owned and what your mom does for a living. He asked about your dad and then he asked how you were connected to Miss Gray and whether or not you had mentioned that you were having any dreams."

"What?" I hear every word Jay says, but my brain is unable to process everything. Why would Hunter be asking all these questions about me? But I think I know the answer. I swallow a lump of dread and feel it settle into my gut.

"I'm not going to try and talk you out of going because I think you're right. You need answers. And you owe it to Miss Gray. But Felix, we need a plan because you were right. Hunter is dangerous, and he knows your secret."

Chapter Thirteen

Midnight Plans

I need more time.

Jay wants to download blueprints of the Muridae house and execute a three-step plan, and I want to bust down the door with a flaming ax. Neither is possible. Plus there's the entire "I'm supposed to be in my room resting" bit, and I'm sure I've nearly run out of time.

We decide the best course of action is for me to head home and wait until late tonight. Jay will meet me at midnight and help me find an easy entrance or open window to the house. From there, I will sneak inside, find Miss Gray, and bust her out. Hopefully without waking anyone up. I change back into the cat, leaving Jay's clothes in a puddle around me. He offers to attach my collar, but I meow at him in response. No sense in getting it on when I'm just going to have to turn human again for dinner with Mom.

Jay promises to see me at midnight, and I hurry back through the garage and across the street without anyone noticing. I've just finished putting on basketball shorts and a fresh T-shirt when Mom calls up that dinner is ready. I stuff my talisman and the collar back under the mattress and make my way downstairs.

Mom is on the phone when I enter the kitchen. She waves at me to set the table, but my ears prick at the sound of my name. With some concentration, I'm able to hear the phone conversation as clearly as if I were sitting on the line with them. Cat hearing is so cool.

"Well, I'll certainly ask him."

"Please see that you do. That woman may be odd, but she is a woman of habits, and it's been three days since I've seen her in her herb garden."

Mom lowers her voice even more, likely worried I'll get scared about such scary news. "Like I said, I'll speak to Felix about this. Maybe she went on a trip, and he just didn't mention anything to me."

"Maybe," Mr. Brewer responds. "I haven't noticed that cat of hers hanging around either."

They hang up shortly after. I'm sipping a glass of water at the table when Mom comes in with a hot bowl of chicken and rice soup.

"How are you feeling?" She looks worried. Probably because of my strange new illness and the upsetting news about Miss Gray. I wonder what she would think if she knew how much actual danger I was in, and I make a vow never to tell her.

"I feel good. I think that nap was just what I needed!"

"You shouldn't nap when you might have a concussion." She frowns as she pushes the bowl closer to me, urging me to eat.

"Well, I fell asleep reading."

The corners of her mouth pull up slightly. "Well I hope some of that reading was homework."

Yeah, right.

"Felix, did Miss Gray mention going out of town?"

This is it. I've been debating about what to say.

"Yes," I lie.

"She has?" Relief sweeps across Mom's face. "Oh, that's wonderful. I mean, good. Good. Where did she go?"

"Umm, to see her mom."

"Her mother?" Mom exclaims.

I can't blame her. Miss Gray is really old, probably older than my grandparents. "Er, yeah. She's umm, really old. So Miss Gray said she needed to visit. Oh, and umm, she took her cat."

I scarf down the remainder of my dinner and leave for my bedroom, using homework as an excuse. I'm not sure if Mom actually believes I'm going to get a start on homework, but she wishes me good night and reminds me to brush my teeth before she settles on the couch and starts up her recorded television shows. The good news is that Mom is distracted. The bad news is sometimes Mom will catch up on her show and binge past midnight. Hopefully that's not the case tonight because I can't be late. Now is my time to use my abilities to do something heroic. I am going to rescue Miss Gray, and with her and Jay's help, I will take down a family of hunters. It's all happening in just a few hours.

I got so bored waiting up for midnight that I actually did start my homework. No wonder I fell asleep.

Once again, I'm in the dream maze, only this time the maze is different. Instead of plain sterile white, the walls drip with a dark, sticky substance that could be tar, but I'm not getting close enough to find out. Whatever the stuff is, it stinks worse than Hunter. It pulses and forms bubbles as it oozes toward the floor.

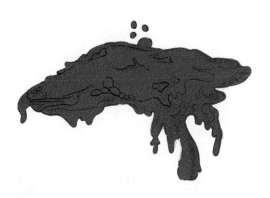

"Hey! Fashion Frills."

"Ethan?" I turn around to face him. "What are you doing here?"

He shrugs. "I dunno. This is your dream." He looks around and seems to notice his surroundings for the first time. "Weird."

"Is this real?" I ask him. "Like are you somewhere dreaming too? Are we actually here?"

He laughs, and the sound is eerily familiar, like the sound from the rat. "What kind of a question is that? I think I'm here because I have a message for you."

"A message?" The goo oozes faster, dripping from the ceiling and running down the walls like cake batter. The smell makes me want to gag. "What is it?"

Ethan rushes forward and grabs my wrist. His grip is impossibly strong.

"She's coming. Run."

The buzzing alarm sounds in my ear, and I fumble to turn it off before Mom takes notice and wonders why I've set an alarm for midnight. The house is quiet, and it seems I might be lucky enough to have a snoring parent. I don't need any supplies since I will change into the cat, but I grab a flashlight just in case Jay needs one. I open the window and chuck the flashlight and a change of clothes outside before I shimmy down the tree in cat form. I might have been just as quick as a human; I can't seem to figure out the downward climb.

Once I'm out of the house and positive that Mom is still sleeping, I turn back into a human and gather my belongings: collar, flashlight, and sneakers. Because why bother to put socks on when they're just going to come off again. I dart across the street toward Jay, who's waiting for me just outside his bedroom window.

"Are you sure you want to do this?" he asks. He closes the window behind him and takes the offered flashlight.

"I don't have a choice." I hand him my collar with the attached talisman and transform again.

Jay snaps on my collar and nods once he's done. "Okay. Let's do this."

We creep among the shadows until we are at the fence line of Hunter's house. The house is dark except for a dim light coming from the living room, possibly from a small lamp or the television being left on. I hop over the fence and land in the soft grass below, waiting for Jay to do the same. His climb over is painstakingly slow, and it takes everything in me not to claw at his sweatpants to get him to hurry. Once we're both over, we go to the north side of the house, the side farthest from the living room.

Just as we hoped, there's a kitchen window.

Jay slides the window open so slowly, I think I might die from the anticipation. When it's finally open, I give myself one final chance to talk myself out of this. But all I can think about is Miss Gray. I have to do this. It's now or never.

I jump up through the open window and into the Muridae house.

Chapter Fourteen

Curiosity Killed the Cat

The house seems normal aside from the overwhelming stench. Like Hunter, the aroma is complex. Both horrifying and intoxicating. Aside from the smell, the kitchen looks like any other kitchen. There's a toaster on the counter and a fancy cheeseboard. There's some soft murmuring in the background, confirming the television is, on somewhere, but otherwise the house seems quiet.

Still, I'm on high alert. Just because Hunter and his family don't appear to be home doesn't mean that they aren't. I begin to explore the house, on the lookout for any clues to Miss Gray's whereabouts. The kitchen, dining room, and living room are all empty. Boring, too, filled with normal furniture and family photos. Nothing out of the ordinary.

I jump onto the mantel to get a better look at some of the photos. Hunter was telling the truth when he said his family moved around a lot. Either that or they really enjoy to travel. There are pictures of them everywhere: big cities, mountain cabins, a jungle tree house, and each picture showing Hunter and his parents cheesing at the camera. They look so normal . . . but I know they're not.

The main floor proves empty, and I'm faced with the decision of whether to explore downstairs or upstairs for Miss Gray. Upstairs, the smell is stronger, likely in their rooms. Downstairs, the basement provides a perfect hiding spot for kidnapped old ladies. I raise my nose to the air, sniffing softly, but all I can smell is Hunter magnified. I patter down the stairs and into the basement.

Part of me has been holding out hope that I am wrong about Hunter and his family. That hope dies once I am in his basement. The finished level of the house was redesigned into a sort of prison or maybe some sort of funky dog room, but Hunter and his family don't own any dogs.

One wall of the room is lined with huge kennels. Each kennel is made of silver metal wiring and large enough to hold a person, but they are all empty. There is no sign of Miss Gray. The opposite end of the room is something even more bizarre. The entire wall is lined with weapons. Literally every weapon I can think of and more that I didn't even know existed. An impossible armory, done entirely in miniature. There is even tiny armor. It is somehow menacing and adorable at the same time. What do they do with these things? Is Mr. Muridae into tiny model action figures? I have an uncle who spends hours and hours replicating old battles. Maybe it's like that? I shake my head to clear it. So far there's no sign of Miss Gray, and I've only been left with more questions instead of answers. I need to finish my search and get out of here.

I'm halfway back up the stairs when I notice the smell has gotten stronger. I tense as I get closer, straining to hear anything above the low hum of the television. Do I detect breathing? Someone shushing another? There's only one way to find out. I continue my ascent, senses on high alert and ready to spring into action.

The smell intensifies, and I reach the top of the stairs ready to fight. A trio of rats greets me: one brown, one white, and one white with brown spots.

"Hello, Felix," says the white rat. "We've been expecting you."

Chapter Fifteen

The Cat's Out of the Bag

I hiss. I don't want to, but I do. My back arches and I hiss again, yowling for good measure.

"I told you. He's dangerous. Look at him!" The spotted rat pulls a tiny dagger strapped to his side. "Say the word, Mom, and I'll skewer him."

"No one is skewering anyone," the white rat says with a stamp from her tiny foot. "Hunter, put away your dagger. Now."

"But, Mom, he—"

"Now!" The rat stamps her foot again, and as she does, her entire body shoots toward the ceiling, growing and stretching and transforming into a human as quickly as I can blink. Which I then do several more times to make sure I'm not seeing things.

"I'm sorry, Felix, you must think us terribly rude. But, you

93

know old stereotypes." She shrugs as if that explains everything. "Now remember, Hunter, cats don't have the gift of tongues as we do. Poor Felix was just trying to communicate, now weren't you, dear? Why don't you change back, and we'll all just have a nice chat."

The brown rat changes next, stretching into a giant man with huge muscles and a burly beard. "Well go on, son. You heard your mother."

The spotted rat sighs, but seconds later, Hunter stands in its place. Like his parents, Hunter is dressed in athletic gear, lightweight pants, and hiking boots.

"It's okay, Felix. We just want to talk."

I don't know what to do. I definitely don't want to change in front of them and admit my secret, but if I smell anything to them like they do to me, then the cat's already out of the bag. And the fact that they literally just called me by my name. I let out one long meow to let them know my intense displeasure and then I run for the kitchen and escape out the window. Jay huddles just outside, and he falls to the grass when I land in front of him.

"Oh, good! I heard voices and— " He stops when he realizes I'm clawing at the collar around my neck.

He removes it for me, and I immediately transform back into a human. I'm pulling on the basketball shorts when Hunter calls out the window.

"Felix? Are you still out there?"

Jay's eyes widen, but I shake my head, telling him to stay put. I need him on the outside, just in case.

Slowly, I rise to my feet, clutching my T-shirt in my fist.

"Are you okay? Can you come back inside? We just want to talk. I'm sorry I threatened to stab you. Don't you want answers?"

Jay grabs my hand and tries to pull me back, but I shake him off. I might be crazy, but Hunter is right. I need answers. Starting with a big one.

"Okay," I said. "I'll come inside. Why don't you come around and open the front door?" That way Jay has plenty of time to make a run for it.

"Fine. It's open. Come on in." Hunter disappears from the window, and I shoo Jay off, promising that I will be okay. I just wish I could feel as confident as I sound.

Hunter is standing in his doorway by the time I make it to the porch. Once again, I'm aware of the fact that he is fully dressed, right down to his shoes. Just like his parents were.

"Umm, you guys get to keep your clothes when you change?"

"You can't?"

Well he doesn't have to make me feel bad about it, sheesh.

I must be getting used to the smell because when I get back in the house, it's not as bad.

"How long have you known?" I ask him.

"How to change with my clothes? Bro, since I was, like, five. Naked bottoms are less cute after you're a toddler. I could teach you, if you want."

"No. I mean, yes! Definitely. I need to learn that yesterday. But no, I meant how long have you known that I'm . . . that I can—"

"That you're a werecat? Umm, since we first met.

Actually since we moved in. I could smell you from across the street. You stink."

"I stink? No, you. You're the one who . . ." I trail off at his laughter. "Okay fine. I get it. You're super smart, and you've known all along that I'm a werecat because you're a . . . you and your family are . . . What are you guys? Did your entire family get scratched by a rabid radioactive rat or something?"

"What? No. Dude, that's offensive. The Muridae family comes from a long line of wererats, a very proud family tradition."

"So everyone in your family is a rat?" I imagine his family hosting a reunion full of rats. Mom would die.

"Most of us, yeah. So umm . . . who scratched you? Not your mom, I take it, because she wouldn't have waited so long. You don't seem to know anything."

"Hunter Elijah Muridae. You watch your mouth." Mrs. Muridae places a gentle hand on my shoulder, and it's an effort not to flinch at her touch. I guess I'm still a bit freaked that just moments ago they had all been rats. "I'm sorry, Felix. Hunter needs to remember that people are different. And that Weres come in all shapes and forms, each with a wide and varied culture— " She notices Hunter mimicking her and slaps the back of his head. "Now, Felix, why don't you boys settle into the living room, and I'll bring us some snacks. Do I need to call your mother and let her know you're here?"

"Umm, please don't."

She laughs and gently nudges my shoulder in the direction of the living room. I follow Hunter and take a seat beside him on the couch, mostly because I can't think of anything else to do. We sit in silence for several moments before Hunter breaks the quiet with a snort of laughter.

"What's so funny?"

"You. You mean to tell me," he says between shouts of laughter, "that you lose your clothes every time you shift?" His laughter is loud and obnoxious, and there's a slightly familiar quality to it that I just can't place. "Here, I'll explain," he says once he finally stops laughing.

Hunter talks for a bit, but it's hard to follow or maybe he's not a good teacher. Something like holding your power and envisioning yourself giving it to your clothes and then asking your clothes to become a part of you . . . or something like that. I think that's going to take some practice, but it's definitely the most useful thing I've learned tonight.

Mrs. Muridae returns with a tray laden with food. There are peanut butter and grilled cheese sandwiches. Smoked fish spread with crackers. Popcorn and glasses of milk and hot cocoa. My stomach growls, and I don't have to be asked twice before helping myself to some snacks.

Mr. Muridae grabs a handful of sandwiches and excuses himself to bed. I can't say I'm sorry to see him go. That guy is scary with a capital S. I'm still not sure how such a big dude can shrink down to rat size. Hunter watches me with a guarded expression.

"So, you were all, umm, just born this way?" Miss Gray had hinted at other Weres, but I never really got past the idea of anything other than a werewolf. She certainly never mentioned rats.

"Yes, dear." Mrs. Muridae takes a seat in the recliner across from me. "There are three types of Weres. Those who are born into, like my family. Those who are made, like you, I presume?"

I nod.

"Mm, yes. Those made will have a talisman, usually. A way to harness the power. And then, of course, there are those who are cursed."

"Werewolves." Hunter says the word with so much venom, it is as if the word itself is cursed.

"Yes, wolves." Mrs. Muridae shudders and blows on her mug of cocoa. "Dreadful creatures. Poor, wretched things." She looks away for a moment, and Hunter fists his hands in his lap. His jaw works hard, and he's clenching his teeth so tightly, his face practically vibrates.

I wonder if something terrible happened to them involving werewolves, but I think better than to ask.

"So, Felix." Mrs. Muridae's voice is laced with false cheer. "How long since your induction?"

"Oh, umm." My hand falls from its path to my mouth, and I set the peanut butter sandwich down. "I guess about a month now."

Mrs. Muridae gasps.

"A month? Seriously? No wonder you didn't know how to change with your clothes." Hunter snorts. "You're basically a baby!"

"Hunter!"

"Sorry, Mom." He doesn't look sorry, though, just

amused. "So then who changed you? Oh. Miss Gray." He nods. "Makes sense."

Miss Gray! I'd gotten so wrapped up in my discovery that I completely forgot to ask about her.

"How did you know about Miss Gray? Did you do something to her?" I jump to my feet, and the peanut butter sandwich falls from my lap to the floor. I regard my cocoa with suspicion, but I don't feel drugged or anything.

"Oh dear. Please relax, Felix. Our kind doesn't mix very well when there are heightened emotions. We don't want to mess with your impulse control. I'll explain everything I can."

She's right. Already their smell seems to intensify, and I have a strong desire to knock all the cups off the coffee table. Somehow, I'm able to calm my breathing until I can sit back down. I pick up the sandwich and place it back on the table; it's more than a bit smooshed.

"Sorry," I mutter, and I'm not sure if I'm apologizing to Mrs. Muridae or the sandwich.

"Now then," Mrs. Muridae begins, "I've sent Hunter with an invitation for a formal meet and greet to the home of your Miss Gray for the last two days, and she has not been home. Are you saying she's missing?"

"Yes. And if you haven't taken her, then I don't know where she is."

"It's not possible she would have left without . . ." She trails off when she notices me shaking my head. "Well then, this is most upsetting. But not to worry. Mr. Muridae is well-respected in the wererat community. We'll get our ears to the ground and find out what we can right away. We'll have your Miss Gray found in no time."

"Yeah, so long as it's before the lunar eclipse, you have nothing to worry about."

"Hunter," Mrs. Muridae warns.

Talk of the eclipse triggers some memory of warning from Miss Gray, but I can't remember what. I wish I paid more attention. I still can't believe that as much as I've discovered here tonight, the trip has still been a failure. I'm no closer to finding Miss Gray than I was before. In fact, now I don't have a single lead.

Mrs. Muridae stands up and begins to clear the coffee table. "It's a school night, and it's been far more exciting than it should have been. You boys need to get some rest, or you'll be zombies in class tomorrow. Felix, would you like to stay here tonight?"

"I'd better not. Not only will my mom flip out, but I've been having some crazy nightmares lately. I don't want to wake everyone up with my screaming."

Mrs. Muridae goes very still. Hunter chokes on his grilled cheese.

"Felix." Mrs. Muridae's voice rises an octave, the way Mom's does when she calls me down to kill a spider. "Describe these nightmares to me."

"Mom." Hunter sounds scared. "Mom, do you think she's found us?"

"Hunter, go upstairs and wake your father. Felix, tell me about your dreams."

I tell her about the maze, the voices, and the spotted rat. I turn to look at Hunter as I say this last bit, but he's gone upstairs to wake his father.

"What's the message?" she asks.

"What?" I'm still trying to piece everything together. How does Mrs. Muridae know so much about my dream? And why did it scare Hunter? They seem to refer to a woman, perhaps the voice in the dream. Do they know her?

"The message, Felix. What was the message?" Mrs. Muridae advances until she catches my shoulders in either hand. Her grip is strong and frightening and not at all the gentle and tender touch like from before. "Your friends, your visitors, the other people in the dream, they all delivered a message. Now what was it!" She shakes me so hard, my teeth chatter.

"Run. They told me to run!" I wish I'd listened. I struggle to pull out of her grasp, but her grip is too strong.

"Jessica, that's enough." Mr. Muridae rips his wife away from me. I stumble back to the couch, breathing hard. I'm going to get up and run for the front door, just as soon as I can move my legs.

"Oh, Felix. I'm sorry. I'm so sorry." Mrs. Muridae stretches out a hand toward me, but I can only stare at her.

"Hunter, keep an eye on your friend. I'm going to see your mother to bed. Uh, don't worry," he adds. He must have seen the wild panic on my face. "I ain't keeping you here or nothing. Just have to make sure to see you home is all. It isn't safe." He pulls Mrs. Muridae toward the hall, and they disappear upstairs.

"So, umm, sorry about . . . well, all of that. Moms." Hunter lets out a nervous laugh, and I finally realize where I recognize the sound.

"It was you, in my dreams. Well, as a rat anyway."

"Yeah. And you've been in mine. That's what has Mom so freaked out. Well, that and the evil witch who's placed a death curse on our entire family."

Chapter Sixteen

Just a Casual Death Curse

Back up. Evil witches and death curses? What kind of rat family is this? And how are we sharing each other's dreams? That doesn't seem possible, but then again, nothing about my life has been inside the realm of normal lately. I'm not sure which question to ask first, but I'm glad I'm still sitting on the couch.

"So, we'll probably have to move again," Hunter says, breaking the silence.

"Because of the curse?"

"Yeah." Hunter's fingers drum against his knee, and he taps his foot to a sporadic beat. "We can't let her find me or she'll kill me."

"Who?" There's no way Hunter means kill, kill . . . right? Who would want to kill an eleven-year-old?

"I'm not exactly sure." Hunter's voice sounds far away even though he is sitting right next to me. "I've never met her or anything, because, you know, she wants to kill me." He laughs, but I can't smile with him. "We just know that it affects the firstborn in my family. It has for generations. Always the firstborn, and always right after their tenth birthday. She, umm, communicates through your dreams. Every few decades or so, she offers a way out, a chance to break the curse . . . but it's never something easy."

I let his words settle over me. I thought it was rough as a werecat. I can't imagine having a death curse placed on me. But, I've heard her voice in my dreams too. And I never did anything to any witch. Am I cursed too?

"I'm sorry you got dragged into all of this," he says as though reading my mind. "I was so freaked out when the dreams started."

"Yeah, I haven't been a fan. Your mom, she asked about the message from the dream visitors?" And they told me to run, I remind myself. I dart a quick glance at the front door. I could make a run for it now. I doubt he would even try to stop me, but I want answers more.

Hunter nods. "Our dreams are practically identical, and I've been having them for over a year now. Running in a maze with no clear way out, the witch begging to be freed." He shrugs. "Typical stuff, except for then I usually have my cousin—"

"Ethan?"

"Ethan? No! He's, like, barely my cousin. And he's weird." He shakes his head. "No, my cousin Bogglert usually pops—"

"You have a cousin named Bogglert?"

"Yes, not the point. Stop interrupting. So Bogglert typically pops up at the end and tells me it's time to move on. You know, like a warning the witch is getting close. Dad says he used to have similar warnings from the visitors in his dreams."

"Because your dad used to be the one with the death curse before you turned ten."

"Yes, exactly! Hey, you're smarter than you let on, huh?"

I decide to let that slide while I figure out whether I'm offended by it or not.

"But then the dreams changed when we moved here," Hunter continues. "And now, instead of Bogglert, I see this little black cat, and the message is 'Catch the cat.'"

"The cat? As in me? Why does she want you to catch me?" Maybe I should have run. I stand up and inch toward the door.

"I don't know. Normally the messages are friendly warnings. Why would you tell me to catch yourself?" He sighs. "You can go if you want to. I wouldn't blame you. But Dad does want to see you across the street. You know, crazy killer witch on the loose and all."

Right. I guess it can't hurt to wait just another moment. Hunter's dad is big and maybe just scary enough to keep away the witch, though I doubt it.

"So you guys really don't know why you're cursed? How is that possible?"

"Dad says it was something one of my great-great—I dunno how many—great-grandparents did. And until we can break the curse, the firstborn is forced to suffer a life on the run. You either run or die, and the only time the witch stops looking for you—"

"Is after you've had your first kid," I finish.

"Bingo. I present to you the current lucky holder of the Muridae curse."

"But if the curse is only continued by passing it through the bloodline, why don't . . ."

"They just stop having kids altogether? Yeah, the curse doesn't work that way. Magic doesn't work that way. Don't you know anything? Sheesh. Magic is wild and chaotic, and it always finds a way. If the current curse holder doesn't have a kid, it just jumps to the next most appropriate Muridae. Or worse. Dad says our great-grandpa got pregnant and gave birth to my grandpa."

"What!"

"Yup. Anyway, she's after me now and maybe you too? I'm still trying to figure out how you're connected. You and your mom might want to think about getting out of town too."

"What? We're not leaving town. My mom doesn't know about any of this, and if I try to use any of it as an excuse for her to ditch her business and us to move, she's going to think I've gone crazy. Surely there has to be some way to end the curse."

"Well, there is one way . . . maybe. But I'm not going to get my hopes up. We would have to—on the day of true moon's glow, end the curse turned friend to foe. Find the witch with truest heart, and friendship found will mend the part." He recites the last bit like it's a nursery rhyme, which I suppose, to him, it kind of is.

"What was that, like some sort of prophecy or something?"

"I guess? If instead of being some super-cool chosen one, I'm this cursed pathetic mess." He laughs again, and I realize his constant jokes about the curse are his way of coping with it.

"Well, you do get a dagger," I say.

"And a teensy little sword!" We both laugh.

Mr. Muridae clears his throat in a meaningful manner. Hunter takes the hint.

"Oh, umm, good night, Felix. I'll see you at school tomorrow."

I wave goodbye as he heads upstairs to his bedroom. Suddenly I'm exhausted, and the idea of crawling into my own bed sounds amazing. It must be close to two a.m. by this point, so if I go to bed now, I can still catch some quality sleep before our busy day tomorrow. Mr. Muridae escorts me across the street and lingers in the shadows until I wave to him from the safety of my bedroom. I wonder if the witch is truly after me now, too, and what that might mean for my life here. There is some clue hidden in the prophecy, I'm sure of it.

And what about Miss Gray? Is her disappearance connected in all this? How could it not be?

I lie down, and even though my bed is warm and cozy, it is a long time before I fall asleep.

Chapter Seventeen

Witch's Truest Heart

It is a dreamless sleep, and I hope Hunter had the same. I can't say that I feel refreshed in the morning, but considering the fact that I had maybe two or three hours of sleep, I'd say I'm handling things pretty well. I make a mental list of tasks as I brush my teeth and get ready for the day. I'll need to fill Jay in on everything that's happening.

We'll need to get back to Miss Gray's and seriously search the place. There has to be some detail I've missed. I don't see how Miss Gray is connected to the witch or Hunter's curse, but her disappearance is too much of a coincidence to ignore.

After finding clean basketball shorts and a T-shirt, I grab my talisman from inside the pocket of last night's shorts and transfer it over. I replay Mrs. Muridae's words from last night. She seemed to know more about being a werecat than I do. They all did. Another reason I need to find Miss Gray.

"Hey, sleepyhead. Thought I was going to have to come wake you up. Wild night last night?"

For a moment my heart almost explodes out of my chest,

but then I catch the mischievous sparkle in her eyes, and I realize Mom is joking. She doesn't know I snuck out last night, thank goodness!

"Jay was here about twenty minutes ago," she continues. "He was wondering if his cat made its way here? Apparently it went missing last night. He was very insistent I check it wasn't in your room. You were snoring like a grizzly when I went up." Her eyes narrow with a sudden thought. "I hope you're not sneaking that cat back in here. I meant what I said. No pets. I don't want a cat under this roof, not ever."

I resist the urge to roll my eyes. If only she knew.

"When does Miss Gray get back from her vacation?"

I freeze at the question. I forgot all about that lie. At the time, I had been so sure Miss Gray was at Hunter's house that it hadn't seemed like such a lie. What now? I don't want to lie to her again.

Suddenly my talisman grows hot in my pocket, and a familiar stench assails my nostrils. Only, it doesn't smell so bad anymore. Seconds later, the doorbell rings.

Thank you, Hunter!

"Uh yeah, Mom. Soon. Gotta go. Can't be late for school." I rush by her before she can think to stop me and fling open the door. Hunter and Jay stand on the other side.

"You're okay!" Jay says as I step out to join them.

"He wouldn't believe me when I said you were fine. Didn't want to believe the rat part, either, but maybe now you can verify." Hunter rolls his eyes at me and turns to Jay. "I told you, I was kidding when I said I would stab him. Can't you take a joke?" Hunter gestures to Jay and laughs. "This guy."

The three of us mount our bikes and begin the short ride to school. Along the way a plan begins to form. Both times I've gone to investigate Miss Gray's disappearance, I've gone alone.

Hunter suggests I'm dimwitted and missed an obvious clue. Jay's approach is more diplomatic, and he says I could benefit from "a fresh set of eyes." In any case we decide the three of us will go to Miss Gray's after school and give her place a thorough search. Jay has a few more lingering questions about wererats and witch curses, and by the time we answer them all, the late bell rings for homeroom. I scoot in before Mr. Hammond notices.

Mckenna isn't in homeroom—maybe an orthodontist appointment or something—which is just as well because now I can focus on my afternoon plans without a distraction. Seems to me, the most important thing to figure out now is Miss Gray's connection to the witch. Why would they take her now? Does it have something to do with the upcoming lunar eclipse? The rest of the morning passes in a blur, and although I've thought of nothing else, I'm no closer to any answers by the time lunch comes around.

Hunter and I basically spent all of last period dissecting the riddle, but the only thing we can agree on is that it has something to do with a good witch and the lunar eclipse. The problem is there aren't any good witches, according to Hunter. He swears that a witch's favorite pastime is draining the magic out of Weres and drinking their blood. Or maybe that's vampires. Either way, they're no good.

I follow Hunter to our now-usual seats in the cafeteria and notice Mckenna picking at some orange slices. She smiles and waves when she sees me, and I return the wave. I think I might have a goofy smile on my face because Jay laughs and punches my arm knowingly.

"They're talking." Jay starts to make a joke about Mckenna being too smart for me — at least I think that's where the joke is going before Hunter interrupts.

"Felix, you can't. Not with her."

I know you can't call dibs on a person or anything, but I'm not letting Hunter swoop in and be better at this too. Sorry dude, I'm not letting you steal my sort-of girlfriend. I lean over to tell him this, but Hunter's face is pale. He leans back from the table and looks around as if looking for another empty seat.

"Hunter, are you okay?"

"No, don't you smell that?"

Jay looks around as if trying to spot some invisible threat. I raise my nose to the air and give it a big whiff. I smell all the usual cafeteria smells, nothing special. I close my eyes and take another deeper, slower sniff, noting distinctions. The aromas of everyone's lunch, of course, the sharp odor of rubber sneakers and hair gel. I can smell Jay, an odd mix of chocolate, aerosol, and his mother's cooking. And  Hunter, of course — that stench is going nowhere. And just faintly, Mckenna. She smells like sunshine on water and wild strawberries. I have no idea what sort of shampoo makes that smell.

"Felix?" Jay prompts.

"Oh, sorry. No. I don't smell anything. Just you." I look at Hunter and shrug.

He seems uneasy but drops his attention to his cheese sticks.

After a few moments, Hunter ends the silence with a fart loud enough to double as a bugle horn. Several students look over and laugh.

Hunter shrugs. "What? I'm lactose intolerant."

We're still laughing when Mckenna taps me on the shoulder.

"Hey, Felix, I hope I didn't miss anything in homeroom today."

"It's homeroom. What could you possibly miss?" Hunter mutters so softly under his breath that I'm sure I'm the only one who's heard.

"Eh, not much." I can't remember a single detail. I've been so wrapped up in Miss Gray and the witch curse.

"Oh. Well that's good, I guess. We actually picked up my cat this morning. We went yesterday, but then when we got th—"

"Guys! What if we're wrong in assuming the truest heart means good? Maybe it just means honest." Jay smacks the table with the palm of his hand.

"Hey, you might be on to something! Felix?" Hunter lifts his eyebrows at me.

"Definitely. Evil people can be honest. What if it mea—" I'm interrupted by Mckenna tapping my shoulder. I actually forgot she was here in that short moment.

"But Felix. Yesterday, at the shelter —"

"Sorry, Mckenna. We're kind of in the middle of something important."

I can tell I've said the wrong thing. She catches her lower bottom lip between her teeth and nods before mumbling an apology and turning away. Should I go after her? Ethan stands up from the table and gives me a smirk.

"Hey, Mckenna, you heading to Fitz's office? I'll walk you." He tosses his bag over his shoulder and jogs to catch up to her. I strain my cat ears to hear her response.

"Yeah, thanks, Ethan."

"No prob," he replies. "Hey did I hear you got a cat? My sister loves animals. Maybe later I can . . ." He's too far for me to hear anything anymore, and I slouch back against the table with a sigh.

"So what do you think, Felix? Is a witch's diary too crazy an idea or just so crazy it might be exactly the answer?" Jay looks excited. His eyes have that same feverish expression they take on whenever he's killing it on Fortnite. Hunter even looks kind of hopeful. "Because I was thinking," he continues, "when can you be sure if anyone is ever telling the truth? You can't, right? But people don't have to lie to themselves. Well, not in that way anyway. My sister writes in her diary every day. She tells that thing all her deep, dark secrets. Umm, hello? Deep, dark secrets? Meet, truest heart."

"Okay," Hunter says, cracking a smile. "I'll buy it. But where do we get a witch's diary?"

"Well that's the best part. Tell him, Felix." Jay grins from ear to ear.

I don't immediately understand what he means. He stares at me expectantly, waiting on me to deliver the punch line to his grand idea, but I'm drawing a total blank. Why does he think I will know where to find the diary of a witch? Suddenly, I'm smiling too. I don't need to find a diary. I know exactly where one is.

We have to take another look at Miss Gray's grimoire.

Chapter Eighteen

Extra Reading Material

I can't wait for school to end. I consider faking another blackout just to get signed out early, but that will only get me another afternoon at the doctor's office, so it's not worth it. Instead, I stare at the clock and watch the minutes drag on for eternity. Each class seems to take longer than the last, and the only way I survive is because Hunter and Jay seem just as anxious as I am. I think we're all ready to get this over with.

About an hour or so after my brain has transformed into complete mush, the final bell rings, and we are finally released for the day. I make a beeline for our bikes and run into Ethan along the way.

"Watch yourself." He uses his grip on my shoulder to keep me from toppling over. I swear he's grown an inch since yesterday. But he doesn't seem evil at the moment, so I allow the tension to leave my shoulder, and he releases me. "Where are you running off to, anyway?"

"Uh, nowhere. I mean, Miss Gray's house."

He narrows his eyes. "You're missing track practice?

Again? For Miss Gray?" He shakes his head. "And when are we going to talk about setting up time to train for the relay, because—"

"Umm, Ethan, I really can't talk right now."

He sighs. "Fine. Catch you around, Fashion Frills."

At least he's stopped calling me a scaredy-cat.

Hunter and Jay are waiting for me. Hunter plays an imaginary drum solo while Jay reads from his science book.

"Finally," Hunter calls out. He ends the solo with a flourish and straddles his bike. "Are you guys ready to do this?"

There's no going back now.

Miss Gray's house is just as I remember, if not maybe a bit dustier. Jay gets to work, opening drawers and cabinets and even going so far as to go through her trash. He must be channeling his inner private detective. Hunter is extra jumpy, picking up objects at random and giving them a smell before setting them down.

The grimoire remains out on the dining room table. I don't know why I'm nervous. It's not like the book itself is dangerous or anything. It's just some silly old book—that possibly belonged to a witch, and it also holds spells capable of breaking the earth or whatever Miss Gray said. So like I said, some silly old book.

"Is that it?" Hunter eyes it with distrust.

"Yeah." I barely touch the cracked leather of the spine. The book is slightly cool to the touch, rippled with age. Otherwise, it appears completely normal.

"And you're sure Miss Gray isn't a witch?" Hunter asks.

"She's not evil," I say somewhat defensively. I mean, Miss Gray is weird and all, but she's definitely not a bad guy, er, girl . . . bad woman? She's not the villain here.

"Well, I didn't find anything," Jay says from behind Hunter. Hunter is so startled, he squeaks and turns into a rat.

"You guys didn't see that," Hunter says once he changes back into his human form. His cheeks are bright red, but I decide it's polite to ignore that.

After a few more moments of useless looking around, we decide to leave. The only thing worth noting is the book, which Hunter refuses to touch. Jay offers to follow me home to help look at the book some more, but Hunter says he needs to go home and talk to his parents. He's still hoping he can convince them to let him stay in town. I can't believe I'm saying this, but I really hope they let him.

Jay doesn't stay for long. The book probably gives him a headache, too, because after squinting at the same page for over twenty minutes, he announces that he needs to go home and work on his STEM project. I can't blame him. I wish I had something to take my mind off everything. Mom is a bit more needy than usual tonight, but I guess I can't blame her, either, with all my weird behavior lately. I think she's about to faint when I announce that I'm heading up to my room to read a book. Once on my bed, I flip open Miss Gray's grandma-aged book to a page at random. This page has flowers pressed into the seam. They are pale and browned, but I think they might have once been a pretty purple, and there's a lingering odor that is sickly sweet. The words swim on the paper, and no matter how many times I blink, I can't seem to make sense of them.

What is happening to me? Can a person suddenly become dyslexic? Is that even what this is? I press my palms against my eyes, desperate to stop the swirling letters.

Instantly I am taken to the dream world. But I didn't fall asleep, did I?

I am in a four-way intersection, alone but not empty-handed. Somehow, I'm still clutching the book. The walls of the maze are white and stretch as far as I can see in any direction. I strain my ears, waiting to hear laughter or footsteps, or even the voice of the evil witch, but instead there is an endless silence.

Well, if there's no clear way to go, then I guess I'll just move forward. As soon as I take a step, the walls begin to bleed tar again.

"Okay, way to ramp up the creepy level, Miss Evil Ghost Witch Lady." There's no response, so I continue moving forward.

"Hello?" My voice echoes back to me. Okay, just wake up then. This is a dream. You know it's a dream. Wake up.

Nothing happens.

"Hello!" I scream as loud as I can.

"Hello," a familiar voice says from behind.

Slowly, I turn around. A woman stands just a few feet away from me. She is wearing something Mom would wear — heels, pants, and a fancy shirt — and she looks to be around the same age as her. I guess she's kind of pretty-looking, for an old lady.

"Wh—who are you?" I don't want to stutter, but I think

my heart might beat right out of my chest.

I try to take a deep breath, but it gets caught somewhere in my throat at her words. "I think you know who I am. What did you call me? Evil ghost witch lady? It does have a certain ring to it."

"What do you want from me?" I take a small step back from her, but I can tell how pointless the action is. There's nowhere to run.

"Oh, Felix, I'm just scratching the surface of what I want from you." She smiles, and her teeth are filed to sharp white points.

I swallow and wish I had a weapon, any weapon, but all I have is this useless book. So I do the one thing my message has been telling me to do all along. I run down the hall.

The witch's laughter echoes off the walls as she appears in front of me.

"You foolish little kitten. Don't you understand? You can't run from me! This world is

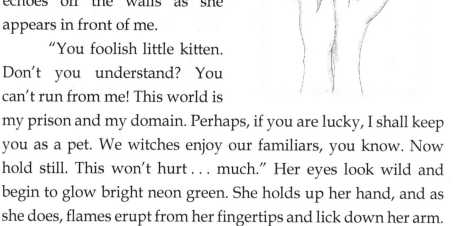

my prison and my domain. Perhaps, if you are lucky, I shall keep you as a pet. We witches enjoy our familiars, you know. Now hold still. This won't hurt . . . much." Her eyes look wild and begin to glow bright neon green. She holds up her hand, and as she does, flames erupt from her fingertips and lick down her arm.

"Stay away from me!" I yell, holding the book up as a shield.

She recoils as if I whipped out a machine gun.

"Where did you get that?"

"You're scared of this?" Realization dawns on me. "Witch's truest heart, right? That's what this is!" I open the book, and it falls open to a page with strange symbols. Line after line in an odd uniform pattern that I realize looks just like the maze.

"Stop it. Stop it before I burn the skin from your spine." The witch screams at me with a fireball hovering over her palm, but she doesn't make a move, and she's not going to. She seems to be too scared of the book.

The letters have finally stopped swirling and form together to create words from a language I don't recognize. I begin to recite the words, not caring that I don't know their meaning. As I say the words, they dance on the page, twisting away and forming a pattern.

The witch screams, and the sound is so terrible that I fall to my knees and cover my ears. But I don't stop reading. I don't stop until I get to the final word on the page, the last word in that twisting, turning pattern, and then everything goes dark.

Chapter Nineteen

A Morning Surprise

It's morning.

I'm still in my clothes from yesterday. Miss Gray's grimoire and my talisman lie on the bed beside me, and somehow it's morning.

Is it over?

Mom opens my door and leans on my doorframe.

"Hi, kid. How are you feeling today?"

"I'm okay." I nod as I take another slow appraisal of myself and my room. Everything seems normal. Is it really only Thursday? It seems like Hunter moved in forever ago and not less than a week.

"No headaches, no bad dreams?"

"Nope. Totally normal."

Mom smiles. "Bravo. Pick up your room so I can vacuum."

I roll my eyes, but Mom is humming as she leaves so I know there isn't any bark behind the order. I wonder if the curse is lifted and if Miss Gray is back home.

I sit up with a big stretch and throw my legs over the side of the bed. I still can't believe I defeated the evil witch with the spell book. It was almost easy. Well, not that easy, I correct myself, remembering her alien eyes and flaming hand. But still, she's gone, and things might finally go my way again.

When I stand up, I realize I've spoken too soon. Things are not back to normal. Somehow, for some reason, I've woken up with a tail.

I'm almost late to school because I can't figure out how to make it go away. I'm still able to change into the cat, but when I shift back, I still have the tail. I eventually just stuff the stupid thing into my sweatpants and run downstairs, barely pausing to shout goodbye to Mom. I run straight to Miss Gray's house, but she's still not home. I don't know why I expected her to be sitting at her dining room table drinking tea.

By the time I've circled back around to the front of the street, Hunter and Jay are waiting for me. I quickly explain the events from last night. Hunter's expressions are a roller coaster ride. I know more than anything he wants to believe the curse is broken, but I get why he doesn't quite take my word for it.

"So what now?" Jay asks as we pedal to school. "We still haven't found Miss Gray."

"And I have a tail."

"And we don't know if you killed the witch who's cursed me."

I don't know how to respond to any of that. Aside from the fact that I need my mentor back, the fact that she hasn't reappeared makes me question whether I actually defeated the evil witch. If I don't know how to explain what happened last night, how can I expect anyone to believe me?

We arrive at school with just a few moments to spare and make plans to discuss Miss Gray and the possible broken curse at lunch. I make it to class and find my seat before Mr. Hammond gets another opportunity to write me up for being tardy.

Mckenna glances at me but then pointedly looks away and opens a book. A textbook even. She could at least try to be convincing if she's pretending to look busy. I have got to fix this.

"Psst. Mckenna." It takes some coaxing, but she finally looks over.

"What, Felix?"

"Umm, hi."

She makes a sound of disgust and looks away.

"No, no! Wait, Mckenna. Pssst. Please."

She sighs and looks back at me. Mr. Hammond continues to drone on with the morning announcements.

"I want to apologize. Can I please just apologize for being a dumb-face jerk?"

"I'm listening," she whispers.

I smile. Okay, good. "I'm sorry. I should have called you last weekend when I said I would, and I shouldn't ever make you feel like you're not important to me."

"Felix, it's fine."

"No, it's not." I hurry on before I lose the nerve. "It's not fine because you are. Important to me, that is." Okay, why is it, like, ten thousand degrees in here? I wipe at the small line of sweat forming on my upper lip. The sweat almost feels stubbly and weird. The seconds stretch on forever before she smiles.

"Thanks, Felix. You're important to me too."

"Really? I mean, that's great. You're great." Shut up, Felix. I try really hard not to grin like an idiot. So I may or may not be stuck with a permanent tail, but at least Mckenna and I are still friends. "Just . . . thanks again for hearing me out. I've just been so distracted with Miss Gray missing and—"

"Miss Gray is missing?" Mckenna's eyes widen in alarm.

Dang it. "No! Not missing. On vacation." I hate that I'm lying again. "I'm, uh, watering her plants."

She nods. "I know you work at her place after school." She throws up her hands as if suddenly remembering something. "That's what I forgot to tell you about yesterday! When I was at the shelter picking up my cat."

I'm in love with a crazy cat lady. Wonderful.

"Does Miss Gray have you watching her cat? And is she missing? Because she's at the shelter! I remember because her calico had, like, the prettiest eyes I . . ."

Mckenna carries on, but I can't hear a word she says. I can't believe it. I can't believe that I didn't let Mckenna finish her silly cat story yesterday. I can't believe that I've been so blind. There weren't any signs of Miss Gray being taken by anything paranormal because she wasn't taken by witches or Weres. She'd been caught by humans.

Miss Gray was at the shelter all along.

Chapter Twenty

Nothing Goes as Planned

The guys can't believe it when I break the news to them at lunch. It was somewhat excruciating waiting until then to tell them, but seeing the expression on both of their faces is priceless. Lunchtime becomes a planning session for a shelter heist, but after the dangerous situations I put myself in over the last week, breaking into a shelter sounds fun.

We make plans to meet after track practice at Hunter's house. Hunter announces that this will be the first time he's ever brought home a human friend, and Jay and I laugh, but I don't think he's joking.

The day continues by with little incident. By the time school ends and track practice rolls around, I'm beat and haven't even started the warm-up yet. Fitz doesn't seem to care that I've been out sick, or maybe Ethan ratted me out. I wonder if Hunter takes offense to that phrase. Fitz makes us all run extra bleachers and seems to take sadistic joy in yelling insults at me.

I consider tapping into the cat for an extra boost of speed, but I'm worried about my control of the cat. I mean, I do currently have a tail tucked into the waistband of my gym shorts.

Finally, practice is over, and I limp back to my bike. Who knew having a tail tucked up in places was chafing? Mckenna sees me and takes pity on me.

"My mom will be here any moment, and we can definitely give you a ride home."

For once I don't have some pressing reason to say no, so I just nod gratefully and take a seat on the curb beside her. Ethan walks by with his bike and comes to a stop in front of us.

"So you made it to practice today?"

"Yeah, someone might have mentioned I was slacking." It takes some effort, but I shove myself back to my feet, careful of my tail.

Ethan nods. "Glad to see you got your priorities straight, Woolfe."

Did he just call me by something other than Fashion Frills?

Don't make it into a big thing, I tell myself. Play cool. But I can't keep the wide grin from spreading across my face.

"First relay practice tomorrow? I have a feeling this new guy will be kind of fast." Of course, that's assuming that Hunter will get to stay in town. I choose to be optimistic though. If a perma-tail is the price I have to pay to keep my new friend . . . well, maybe it's worth it.

Later that evening, Jay and I sit in Hunter's living room while Mrs. Muridae serves us cookies and milk. It takes a bit of work, but I think we're able to convince Hunter's parents to stick around a bit longer. At least until they are sure the witch is still after them.

Mrs. Muridae calls Mom and Jackie—Jay's parents are both working—and gets permission for us to stay for dinner. She claims she is making a big family tradition, but then she just orders pizzas with extra cheese. There is a heated debate over how the heist should be performed. Hunter swears that he can flatten himself to the size of a golf ball and enter through the drainpipe, and Jay thinks there might be some way to hack their security mainframe. I want to suspend myself from the building's roof, but Mr. Muridae puts an end to all that when he comes into the den and announces he just adopted Miss Gray online. We all pile into his truck and drive into town.

The shelter isn't the most impressive building, but that's only if you're not impressed by the smell. Even Jay agrees it's one of the most stinky places in the city. Mr. Muridae parks the car and asks us all to wait outside. I don't like the idea, but he promises to call Hunter's phone if there are any complications. Then he shuts the door and leaves us all behind.

Hunter starts fiddling with the radio. It wouldn't be so bad if he left it on any one station for longer than a second.

I shift in the seat. My tail is in the most awkward spot, and there's just no right way to sit on it without it being a pain. I'm worried the tail might not go away, but I don't say that to Hunter because I don't want him to feel worse than he already does. I mean, I would feel pretty bad if I forced Jay to grow bat wings or something. But then again, Jay might like that.

He suddenly turns off the radio and leans back to face me and Jay. "Do you think the curse is truly gone?"

"I don't know," I answer honestly. "I can't say for sure. One moment I was melting her with some spell, and the next I was awake. Do you think it is? Do you feel any different?"

"I want to believe that it's gone. My parents do, too, more than anything. Felix, if this curse is gone, I can never repay you. You've given me, and my entire family, a new chance at life."

I look away, uncomfortable with his praise, and notice Mr. Muridae walking back to the car, cardboard carrier in tow.

"They're here!"

Hunter scrambles to the back seat to make room.

Mr. Muridae opens the door and places the cardboard carrier on the seat. Jay and Hunter lean to the side to give me space. I peer over the seat and into the box.

"Miss Gray?"

"Meeeeooooooooooowwwwwwwwwwwaaaarrrrrrrrrrrr."

Oh, that's Miss Gray all right, and she is not happy!

128

Mr. Muridae chuckles. "Well we don't need any translation for that. Hold tight, Miss Gray. I'll have you back at home and in your human bed in no time."

It's a joyful ride back home for the most part, except for some random hissing from Miss Gray. Mr. Muridae rolls down the windows, and we all sing along to the radio.

We drop Miss Gray off first. She shoots off up her stairs as soon as I open the door for her. I want to stick around. I have so many questions, but Mr. Muridae insists that Miss Gray needs a night of privacy, so he sends us all home.

Mom is beside herself that Jay and I have a new friend. She says she's looking forward to having the Muridae family over for dinner. I wish more than anything that I could have the pleasure of informing her she would be dining with a family of rats because she would flip.

We talk until I'm yawning, and Mom sends me to bed. She gets no complaints from me, and I shuffle up the stairs and crawl into the sheets with my tail tucked in around me.

I'm dreaming again. The realization hits me with an icy dread. I'm not in the maze though. Instead, I'm standing in a forest clearing. I spin in a slow circle, half expecting the trees to start melting into tar. The forest appears normal, teeming with life and the sounds of birds, squirrels, and other creatures going about their day-to-day business.

Is this a normal dream then? I've never been lucid during my other dreams, but maybe being in the witch's dream world opened up a new ability. How crazy would that be?

I'm just beginning to relax when the forest goes silent around me. Birds stop singing, and even the wind ceases to rustle the leaves. I stop. My heartbeat quickens. This can't be good.

A twig snaps behind me. I turn toward the sound to find the witch. She leans against a tree, smiling viciously. Those teeth are seriously creepy!

"You're alive!"

"Alive?" She chuckles. "Oh, you amusing little boy! Did you think you killed me? So easily?" She shakes her head, and her dark hair spills over her shoulders. "Foolish child, I am one of the ancients. I cannot be dismissed by a mere book."

I shake my head. "B—but . . . the spell. I was hurting you."

"I only made you believe you were hurting me so you wouldn't stop the recitation. You weren't hurting me at all. You were freeing me. And now I'm free from that dreadful prison that's been holding me for centuries."

"But . . . the curse. The Muridae family."

"Oh, I have my plans for them. I have plans for you all."

"No." I shake my head and look around. I need a stick or something to defend myself.

"Don't you see, Felix? You've won nothing. You can do nothing. And my plans have only just begun."

Chapter Twenty-One

Only the Beginning

When I wake up, it's still dark outside, and I've grown whiskers. I pull one out, but it's so painful that I decide I'm either learning to shave or joining the circus. Either way, there is no way I can go back to sleep after that. I fling myself out of bed and pull on some fresh shorts, shoving my tail down behind me. It has a mind of its own, especially when I'm in such an agitated state, but I'm not sure how to change that.

How could I have been such an idiot? Did I really think I was capable of single-handedly defeating a witch? I tear into myself a bit more as I brush my teeth and try to smooth down my bed head. Mom is still snoring, so I leave a note on the coffee machine stating that I went to Miss Gray's to return her key, which finally isn't exactly a lie. Then I grab her grimoire, push my tail back in my pants, and ride to Miss Gray's house.

She answers the door in a flannel nightdress, exactly the kind you would picture old TV grandmas wearing. Except Miss Gray's golden eyes have a feral quality to them, and no self-respecting grandma would ever scowl like this at a kid.

She holds out her hand by way of greeting, and I place the book into her waiting arm. The moment the book is in her hands, the tail and whiskers disappear. My hands fly around to my backside, and Miss Gray gives me a knowing look.

"A borrower's spell. Slowly transforms the thief into a cat, bit by bit, until the item is returned or until they remain permanently a cat. A useful trick." She gestures for me to enter. "I would have thought you learned not to steal from me after the last time." She sighs, but there is no anger in her tone. If anything, now she just seems really tired. Which, I guess I did pound on her door an hour before dawn . . . Sheesh, no wonder she's not my biggest fan.

"It seems you've had an eventful week." The corner of her mouth lifts slightly in a wry smile. "I suppose we both have. Have a seat, and I'll make us some warm milk while you talk."

I fill Miss Gray in on everything, even the details she doesn't ask for like my fight with Mckenna and my odd behavior around Jay. Finally I tell her about the Muridae family and their curse. Miss Gray listens the entire time without any interruptions, and by the time I finish with last night's dream, I can barely hold back my yawns.

"So you and the rat have become friends. Likely, those blackouts stem from unexpected power surges as you age. Oh, I don't think the witch has anything to do with that. And quite frankly, neither does your rat friend, at least not directly. You're a growing boy, Felix. Nearly a teenager, and hormonal. That's why it's so imperative that you stick with your training. You can expect several more power surges as you age."

Awesome. How did I get to be so lucky?

After the long lecture I receive from Miss Gray, I should get a pass on going to school. I'm exhausted and already planning to nap through math class as I leave the house and head up the street to meet the guys.

Jay is in his driveway and notices me. He waves and meets me in the street.

"How is she?" he asks.

I search my brain, at a loss for what to say. I know he's asking about Miss Gray, but when he asks how she is, all I can think of is the evil witch. How do you tell your best friend that you may have just put him and everyone you know in danger?

"Guys! Hey, you guys!" For once, I hear him before I smell him.

Hunter stumbles down his driveway and runs toward us at full speed.

"My parents said we can stay!"

Jay whoops and does a fist pump. "Awesome news."

I can't find it in me to take away his reason to celebrate.

"What made them change their mind?" Jay asks.

"Last night I had another dream."

I turn to look at Hunter, but he's looking at Jay, and neither of them notices my wild expression.

"What dream? What did you—" I try to keep the panic from taking over.

"Guys, I was back in the maze. The maze."

Goosebumps race down my arm.

"Yup, just like before. And all I can do is run through it, stuck as the rat. So I'm thinking, great. Any moment, and the witch will start threatening me again. And then I get to the center of it, and you know what I found waiting for me?"

"Bogglert?" I ask.

"No, a pit full of cheese! It was glorious." Hunter smacks his lips. "I woke up and told my parents, and we all agree. It's a good omen. The curse is finally broken."

Jay gives him a high five, and I stare down at my sneakers.

"Hey, how's your cat sensei?" Hunter asks.

"Yeah, you never got to tell me what she said." Jay looks at me expectantly.

"She, umm . . ." Hunter is the happiest I've ever seen him. How can I take that away from him? "She took away the tail," I admit. The guys start another round of whoops and high fives.

"So everything is finally settling back to normal." Jay grins. "We can all go back to living happy lives."

"With increased training," I say glumly.

"But new friends?" Hunter elbows me. "Although, there is probably one thing we should talk about."

He has no idea just how right he is, of course. We have a

lot to talk about. But I think we could all just use a day of fun. It is Friday, after all.

"What is it?" Jay asks.

At the same time, I ask, "Can't it wait?"

"Wait?" Hunter snorts. "No way. This is a matter of life or death. Best friends have to look out for each other."

I guess he knows the witch is still alive. Well, this makes it easy, or difficult, depending on how you look at it.

"Well, Felix, do you want to tell him, or should I?"

Poor Jay looks so confused. "Tell me what?"

I guess this is it. So much for having a fun Friday.

"Does Felix want to tell you that his girlfriend is a witch?"

Discussion Questions

1. Why is it hard for Felix to trust Hunter?

2. Do you think Felix learned anything about the importance of following rules?

3. Do you think Felix has learned to be a better friend?

4. Have you ever heard the expression, "don't judge a book by its cover?" How does that fit into this story?

Coming Soon:

TALES OF A

SIXTH-GRADE WERECAT

Book 3:

A Familiar Witch

Keep Reading for a Sneak Peek

Chapter One

Which Smell is the Witch?

What do you do when you discover your girlfriend is a witch? Because I can only manage to blink back at Hunter. Jay's eyes are the widest I've ever seen them, but surprisingly, he doesn't look scared. In fact, he looks almost a bit too interested, like he's about to go inside for some popcorn.

"She's not my girlfriend," I finally manage to say. And she isn't, not exactly. I'm not even sure I want a girlfriend, and I especially don't want one who is a witch! A month ago, I was certain witches didn't even exist, and now I'm dating one?

Hunter's expression is grim.

"Sheesh, Felix. We really need to work on your sense of smell." Hunter shakes his head and kicks his leg over his bike.

He's so nonchalant, like he didn't just drop the biggest bomb on me, like announcing that someone is a witch isn't that big a deal. But then again, maybe it isn't to him.

"Wait, so do witches smell funny too? Better or worse than Felix?" Jay still doesn't look concerned. But he's not the one chilling with a witch in homeroom.

"They just smell . . . different. I can't explain it."

"That's lame," Jay says. He frowns down at the blue watch on his wrist. "We have to go or we'll be late." Jay hates being late to school. Not because he's worried his parents will get mad at him, but he actually likes going to school. Sometimes I don't know how we're best friends.

Hunter pedals to catch up with Jay, but I can't seem to find any hustle in me. How can I get my legs to move when all of my energy is focused on keeping my brain from exploding?

Witches exist. Okay, well I did see this one coming . . . sort of. Turning into a werecat will certainly expand the mind to more possibilities. I manage to get my feet moving and follow Hunter's and Jay's retreating forms.

Witches are evil. Another obvious one. I didn't spend the last week running from a crazy witch in the dream world for me not to realize how dangerous witches are.

But Mckenna? A witch? It just doesn't make sense.

Hunter is wrong. He has to be. He has more experience with witches than anyone you know. I try to push away that thought, but it isn't easy. An evil witch placed a death curse on one of Hunter's rat ancestors.

We don't know why, but as far as I can figure, it's best to focus on the few things we do know. Witches don't like rats, and they can place death curses on people. And I don't think death curses are something to mess around with. Poor Hunter and his family have been on the run from the mysterious witch his entire life, moving from place to place whenever the witch got close. Now, his parents have agreed to stay in town, but only because they believe the evil witch was defeated. By me.

I thought she was, too, up until last night when she transported me back into the dream world. I want to believe that it was just a terrible nightmare, my mind processing the events from the last few days, but deep down I know that's not true.

Not only is the witch still very much alive, but she claims I freed her from her prison in the dream world. She said she has big plans for me. I've been working up the courage to confess this to Hunter, but he decided to surprise me with the Mckenna news first. And now here we are. I've lied to basically everyone I know, an evil witch is out trying to kill my friends and possibly me, too, and my almost-girlfriend is a witch.

This isn't the best way to start the weekend.

I wheel my bike up to Tolville Middle School and lock it beside Jay's. There is no sign of either him or Hunter, and seconds later, I realize why.

The late bell. It's going to be a long day.

Chapter Two

Homeroom Horrors

Mr. Hammond is my homeroom teacher. He frowns at my entrance and makes a big show of clearing his throat and glaring at the clock before going back to the morning announcements. Unlike Jay, this is my second tardy of the week. With any luck, I'll manage to get out of here without Mr. Hammond sending a note home for Mom. The problem is that lately I haven't been very lucky.

I have a love/hate relationship with alphabetical order. With the last name Woolfe, I'm always in the back of the line or last to be called. When I discovered Mckenna Watson was assigned the seat next to me, I was thrilled. Now I don't know what to feel.

She smiles at me and I swallow desperately, trying to dislodge the imaginary giant gobstopper that managed to lodge itself in my throat.

Mckenna is really pretty today. I love her long brown hair and freckles. She's also one of the fastest kids in our school, and she's super nice.

And possibly a witch. That gobstopper isn't going anywhere.

"How is Miss Gray's cat?" Mckenna whispers.

I nod slowly.

She giggles. "What does that mean? Is she back at home?"

I nod again and Mckenna rolls her eyes in response.

"Well do you have to work after school today? I was thinking we could have a meeting with the relay team." She leans forward, sticking her leg out as she does, and gestures at her purple sneakers. "I got new running shoes yesterday, and—"

"Miss Watson, please, by all means. I'll wait." Mr. Hammond gives her a pointed look.

Mckenna scowls but turns her attention forward. I've never been so grateful to a teacher in my life.

Mckenna certainly doesn't seem like a witch. She just seems normal. But then again, if she is a witch, wouldn't that be her plan? To hide among normal kids waiting for her chance to strike? I steal a sideways glance at her, but nothing about her outward appearance indicates her to be anything other than a cute girl. I sigh. Maybe Hunter is mistaken. He doesn't have any proof, right? Just that she smelled different or something. Well, that's no reason to suspect somebody of something. And yes, I'm ignoring the fact that, that is exactly what I did last week when I met Hunter.

I wonder what he meant by odd smell. I don't smell anything other than the normal classroom smells: markers, eraser, and Mr. Hammond's sweaty armpits.

I reach into my pocket, and my fingers brush against the

baseball card hiding there. The Jackie Parker Jr. card is my talisman and the only way to hone my werecat abilities. I focus on the cat and take another deep breath. There. I can smell Mckenna, although she certainly doesn't stink. Honestly, she smells kind of great. I think her shampoo is berry-scented, strawberries probably, and there is something else too. Maybe cotton candy? Melting sugar on a hot day? I take another deep breath.

"Are you — did you just sniff me?" Mckenna stares at me, her blue eyes wide with concern.

"No! I . . ." I look around for an answer, but I don't think there's any way to explain myself without coming across as a giant psycho.

Tales of a Sixth-Grade Werecat:
A Familiar Witch

Coming Soon!

Acknowledgments

The biggest of thanks belongs to my readers, without your support this book wouldn't be possible.

Next have to acknowledge the many people who work behind the scenes of this book to make it such a huge success. First off, the biggest thank-you of them all goes to my amazing and talented baby sister, Courtney Landers. Thank you so much for all the long phone calls and intense discussions while we discuss the future of a fictitious eleven-year-old. Now if we can only make our own lives as exciting…

Next, I have to acknowledge Megan Hoffman, my illustrator. I love the illustrations; they made the story come together perfectly. Be sure to follow her on Instagram @mvh_creative!

Another huge thanks to the team at Kingsman Editing, in particular Cayce Martinez, my editor and bestie. Thank you so much for all your help in making this book baby great! Big thanks to Crystal as well as the rest of the behind-the-scenes team.

The cover art was designed by Shivana Brhamadat with sinsvalentine.com with typography by Joel Torres with drivends.com. Joel also designed the trailer if you've seen that floating around.

This book also had many people rooting me on as fan

supporters and I have to say a big thanks to Melisa Jurado and my parents for geeking out over the new direction this story has taken.

I sincerely appreciated everyone who had watched my progression and to all who have followed Felix's story. THANK YOU!!

About the Author

Alexis Marrero Deese is an avid reader of fantasy. Her favorite authors include Brandon Sanderson and Leigh Bardugo. She graduated from the University of South Florida with a Bachelor's Degree in Creative Writing and is the author of the Dance of the Elements series and *Tales of a Sixth-Grade Werecat*.

When she isn't writing, Alexis is probably cooking an elaborate feast, riding unicorns, slaying monsters or simply curled up with a good book.

For more information and for a list of her other titles please visit www.amdeese.com

About the Illustrator

Megan V Hoffman is a proud graduate of the University of South Florida, College of the Arts. She is a painter, illustrator, and art teacher. She is just happy to be here. For more information on her upcoming projects, follow her on Instagram: @mvh_creative.

CPSIA information can be obtained
at www.ICGtesting.com
Printed in the USA
BVHW072211150522
637101BV00002B/181